Still *Wifey* Material

www.melodramapublishing.com

Library of Congress Control Number: 2007943731
ISBN-13: 978-1934157107
ISBN-10: 1934157104
First Edition: November 2008
10 9 8 7 6 5 4 3 2

Still Wifey Material

A NOVEL BY

Kiki Swinson

Starting Over
(Kira Speaks)

After two long weeks of unnecessary drama, and of mourning the deaths of Quincy, Rhonda, and my grandmother, Nikki and I made up. She took the death of my grandmother pretty badly, though. I was broken up about it myself, but Nikki and my grandmother grew very close after my supposed death. Having to go on in life without my grandmother was going to be a very difficult journey for her, which was why I suggested that she and I move to Houston, Texas. She was kind of hesitant at first, but after I told her how cheap the real estate was there and that we could open up a brand new hair salon and make plenty of money, she jumped at the opportunity.

While I got on the phone with a real estate agent, Nikki put in for a transfer with her probation officer, Maxine Shaw. Maxine gave her some static in the beginning, but ended up approving it. I tied up the loose ends with the salon and sold everything. I hit Rhonda's mother off with a little cushion for the kids, since they were my godchildren, and packed my bags. After saying our goodbyes to Nikki's parents, we were out of there.

Life in Houston was a bit different. There were a lot of people with dough living out there, and if they didn't have any money, they looked like they did, so I had to step up my game. I purchased a beautiful

twenty-five-hundred-square-foot brick home in the gated community
of Sonoma Ranch Estates with three bedrooms and a huge backyard
for less than one hundred seventy-five thousand dollars. I went to
the nearest Lexus dealership and traded in my old Lexus for a 2008
Matador Red Mica LS 460 with tan leather interior. The shit was so
hot, and not only that, but I looked good in it. Nikki must have had
the same thoughts as me, because she pulled out her checkbook and
stroked a seventy-five-thousand-dollar check to the same salesman I
used, so she could buy the exact same car I bought. Hers was black with
gray interior. They even threw in a set of custom rims. You should have
seen her face after she handed the check to the man. It was like she was
trying to prove something to me.

After the salesman took her money and left to speak with his sales
manager to process her deal, I pulled her aside and asked her where she
was going to get the money to cover the check.

"Why are you worried about it? I got this," she replied, and then
she smiled and started to walk away.

I grabbed her arm. "Why you got to walk off? This is serious. These
salesmen ain't got time for games. They are expecting every number you
wrote on that check to be in that account," I warned.

"And it is," she said, getting frustrated. "I took two-hundred-
thousand from Syncere's stash while he was locked up. That's why the
nigga tried to kill me."

"Oh really?"

"Yep, I sure did," she said with a smirk. "All the shit I took from
him, I deserved every penny." And with that said, she scooted toward
the accounting office.

I stood there in disbelief because in all honesty, I didn't buy one
word she had said. She was one timid-ass bitch, and I knew how afraid
she was of Syncere, so she would not have taken anything from his
crazy ass. Besides, right before we left Virginia, there was some talk on

the streets that Quincy had been hit up for a large sum of cash either before he got killed or right after. Since Nikki told the police that she was the one who found his body tortured to death, I figured she had to be the one who clipped him. When I asked her about it a while back, she denied it, so I left it alone and didn't bother to mention it to her again.

If you wanted my opinion, I could have cared less if she took his money, because I had my own. As a matter-of-fact, between the five-hundred-thousand-dollar insurance check I got from Ricky's death, the one-hundred-fifty-thousand-dollar insurance check I got from a policy I took out on my grandmother years ago, and the little bit of money I got from selling my business, I was going to be set for a while.

As far as Nikki was concerned, she had a few plans of her own. None of them had been brought into manifestation, but she kept reminding me constantly of how she wanted to open up a salon of her own, so it wouldn't be long before she decided to branch off and do her own thing. Speaking of which, a few days after Nikki and I rode away from the dealership with our new whips, I stumbled across the perfect location for my salon while I was cruising around the uptown district of Houston. Since it came at a really good price, I snatched it up the very next day. It only took us about a month to open the shop, which I named Creative Images, and we rented out two of the other four booths we had to some well-established hair stylists from the area.

That was the easy part. The hard part came after we finally opened the salon's doors. Stylists from other salons in the area started hating on us because we took their clients. When I tell you that the chicks out there were vicious, believe me! A lot of those hoes had a lot of mouth. In fact, there were three loudmouthed Nigerian chicks who braided hair in a shop right next door to us. They were always getting into it with Nikki about the parking spaces outside, since we only had eight parking spaces in the side lot that we all had to share. It seemed like every time Nikki and I turned around, their customers were taking up all the damn spaces.

One day I made a trip over there and had a few words with the owner, Sophie. Sophie was one ugly bitch, but you wouldn't be able to tell her that. She wore traditional African clothing and wrapped her hair like she was a goddess or something, but she was ghetto as hell.

When I walked into her shop, everybody, including all five of her clients, turned to face me. It was no secret why I was there, so I walked over to Sophie, threw my hands in the air, and said, "I know you know why I'm here."

Sophie's big, Amazon-looking ass just stood there with a handful of synthetic braiding hair in her hand and gave me the stupidest expression she could muster. She tried to act like she had no idea why I was there, so I played along because if she wanted to act stupid, then I was more than willing to treat her that way.

"Who in here drives a white Ford Explorer and a blue Toyota Camry?" I asked.

"I drive the Camry," one client yelled out.

"I'm driving the Explorer," one of the Nigerian hair braiders said.

"Well, y'all are going to have to move them because I have a couple of customers at my shop that don't have anywhere to park."

Both women sighed heavily as if I had just interrupted them, but they got up and grabbed their car keys from their handbags. I smiled at them both and said, "Thank you."

On my way out I heard Sophie mumble something under her breath and then everybody laughed. Her English was really off, but I still understood some of the shit she said. As much as I wanted to turn around and ask them what was so damn funny, I told myself that it would be a waste of time. I held my head high and kept it moving. In this day and age, you couldn't always feed into drama, especially with the hoes over there, because Nikki and I were from out of town and we could not get caught up in their bullshit. Moreover, we had more business than they did, so the tension between my front door and theirs was thick enough to cut with a knife.

About two weeks ago, Alana, one of Sophie's stylists, arrived one morning and saw Sophie's husband trying to holler at Nikki. When Sophie got wind of it, she walked into our shop and immediately wanted Nikki to tell her what her and her husband's conversation was about. Nikki stood her ground and told Sophie that she was the wrong person to be talking to.

"What do you mean, you are the wrong person? Weren't you the one smiling in my husband's face?" Sophie asked, irritation stamped across her broad face.

"Sweetie, I smile in a lot of cats' faces, so you're gonna need to step to him about this one," Nikki retorted. She turned her back and walked to our back office.

Sophie said a few things in her native language and stormed out of our shop, which was fine with me because she got the hell out of my face. After she left, I walked back to our office and screamed at Nikki about fucking with that bitch's husband, because I didn't travel all the way out there to create a whole new set of problems. And I let her know this shit too.

"What the fuck is up with you and that bitch's husband?" I yelled. "You know I'm not trying to get into unnecessary drama! So, you need to correct that bullshit and do it like yesterday!" I warned.

"He came on to me first!" Nikki protested.

"So what!" I sighed heavily. "You see how stupid she'll act behind him, so back the fuck up and get your own man!"

"Come on now, I don't even like that ugly-ass nigga!"

"Well, tell him that the next time he approaches you, because we don't need that bitch running over here every time she finds out he was in your face. We are running a business here, so we do not need the drama."

"Yeah, a'ight," Nikki said and went on about her business.

That day was pretty upsetting for me, so upsetting that I had to take a time-out to pop two Tylenols because I had gotten one bad migraine. God knew that when I got a migraine, it damn near killed me, so I made it my business to keep the tension down between Nikki and those Nigerian chicks.

On another note, I still had to get my doctor to diagnose the real reason why my migraines started. I kept telling the son of a bitch that I got shot a while back and that might be the cause, but he kept telling me some other bullshit. At that point it really didn't matter, just as long as he found me the right medication to contain that shit before I went off the deep end.

❦

Later that night, Nikki and I decided to eat at the Applebee's restaurant on Loop 610 West, which was only ten minutes away from our house. While we were being escorted to our table, we passed three cats at the bar. All three of them were handsome in their own little way. You could tell by their mannerisms and loud, boisterous chit-chat that they were average dudes. The one at the end of the bar tried to get us to chill with them, but we declined. After we were seated, the guy from the bar who invited us to sit with him walked over and paid us a visit.

Nikki saw him coming. "Oh, Lord, here comes your boyfriend," she mumbled.

I looked up, and there he was, approaching our table. To prevent the guy from feeling awkward, I smiled and greeted him after he said hello.

"Why y'all eating alone?" he asked.

I took a look at him from head to toe and when I tell you that homeboy looked good enough to eat, believe me, he did. He had to be every bit of 215 pounds and about six feet three. He was stacked up in all the right places, and was kind of handsome. He reminded me of the NBA basketball player Carmelo Anthony with his long cornrows. The guy wore a dark blue, button-down shirt with a small RocaWear logo stitched over his heart and a dark blue pair of RocaWear jeans. The crisp white Air Forces he had on his feet made him look like a young boy with new money.

"Eating alone gives us time to catch up on some girl talk," I finally answered.

He smiled. "Well, that's all good, and I'm gon' give you your space so you can do that. But, can y'all beautiful ladies please tell me your names?"

I smiled back and then Nikki and I both introduced ourselves. He told us his name was Jamal and that he and his other friends lived in the area, so they decided to come out and get a few drinks.

"What are y'all drinking?" Nikki interjected.

"Well, I was drinking on a couple of beers. But my homeboys are sipping on some harder shit."

While Nikki and Jamal carried on their conversation, our waitress came over and took our order. As soon as she left, another one of Jamal's friends came to our table. I was really not in the mood to entertain anyone at that point. All I wanted to do was sit down and eat in peace, especially after the day I had. It didn't matter how I felt, though, because Jamal's friend was coming over, and from the look on his face, he was confident that no one was going to stop him. I took a deep breath and exhaled. *Be nice*, I told myself.

"How y'all ladies doing?" Jamal's friend asked as he extended his hand first to me, then to Nikki.

"We're doing fine," Nikki and I said in unison.

"Is Jamal over here bothering y'all?"

"No, he's fine," I said. Jamal was talking to Nikki, not me, so I was fine with it.

"What's your name?"

"Kira," I replied with disinterest, but he didn't get the hint because he took a seat in the booth next to me. I immediately buried my head in my hands.

"Hi, Kira, I'm Dexter. Are you all right?" He looked concerned.

I lifted my head. "No, I think I'm coming down with a headache," I lied.

"Oh, I'm sorry! Would you like for me to massage your temples?" He reached for my head.

I was utterly appalled, and my expression showed it. "No, I'll be fine. Thank you." I looked over at Nikki, who looked like she was about to burst into laughter.

Dexter gazed back and forth between me and Nikki. "Did I miss something?"

I tried to keep a straight face as I replied, "Sweetie, please don't get offended, but I am not in the mood for a lot of chit-chat tonight. I am tired, and all I want to do is relax and eat my food in peace, if you don't mind."

Dexter slid out of the booth and stood. "Damn, it's like that?" he snapped.

I shook my head in disbelief and turned my attention to Nikki and Jamal.

"Fuck you, bitch! You ain't all that, anyway," Dexter said and stormed off.

Shocked by his outburst, I turned back around and watched him as he headed back over to the bar. Nikki looked at me and said, "Did that whack-ass nigga just call you a bitch?"

I chuckled a bit, just to keep from going off. "Yes, he did." I was still looking in his direction.

"Don't pay him no mind," Jamal interjected. "He's drunk."

"He just disrespected my cousin, so do you think we care about that nigga being drunk?" Nikki snapped.

"It's OK, Nikki. Don't get all worked up behind that loser! I mean, look at him, and look at how he's dressed. Who wears tight-ass Levi jeans with a pair of Timbs and a white T?"

Nikki burst into laughter, but Jamal didn't think it was funny.

"Come on, now, don't diss my homeboy like that," he begged.

"Fuck your homeboy!" Nikki told him.

Taken aback, Jamal got up from the booth and said, "Let me get away from over here before I curse your stupid ass out."

"Yeah, please carry your dumb ass away because if you think you gon' curse me out, and I'm just gonna sit here and take it, you got another thing coming!" Nikki roared at him, rolling her eyes and giving him much attitude.

"Yeah, whatever!" Jamal replied and walked off.

"Whatever, my ass! Got the nerve to be walking around here, wearing a knock-off Movado watch like you paid a lot of money for it."

I grabbed Nikki by her arm. "Girl, don't stoop to his level."

"I'm not, but can you believe those fools? Coming over here, invading our space like they got it like that. What's wrong with those idiots?"

"Nikki, let's just drop it. They're back at the bar now, so let's just enjoy our meal so we can get out of here."

"I don't even want to eat here anymore." She looked around for the waitress.

"Whatcha trying to do, get our food to go?"

"Yep. I am not trying to be in this place any longer than I have to."

I totally agreed with her. We finally got our waitress's attention and told her we wanted our meals to go. She had our food packaged up and our check on the table in less than five minutes flat. Nikki and I were very pleased, pleased to the point that we tipped her ten dollars each before we left the restaurant. On our way out, Jamal gritted on us like a little bitch, but we ignored his silly ass and kept it moving. Niggas like him and that other clown Dexter were the type of cats that couldn't take it when a chick dissed them and told them to beat it. They ran up on the right two chicks tonight, though. Fuck 'em both.

On our way home, I stopped by the Texaco service station so I could pick up a couple packs of Tylenol to stop this headache I had coming on. Nikki stayed in the car while I went into the little convenience store. It only took me about three minutes flat to get in the store and out, so I was happy about that. Time was of the essence, and I was ready to go home and relax.

When I walked back to my car, I noticed Nikki leaning out of the passenger window, grinning all up in this guy's face. He was pumping gas only two feet away from her. He was tall and dark-skinned with high cheekbones. His features were very distinguished, and his accent immediately led me to believe that he couldn't be from any other continent but Africa. Where in Africa, I couldn't tell you, but I was sure Nikki knew.

I settled into the driver's seat. Nikki looked back at me and smiled, and then she took the liberty to introduce me to Bintu, her new foreign friend. I politely smiled at him and said hello. Bintu returned the greeting and stepped aside so that he could introduce me to his brother Fatu, who was in the passenger seat of Bintu's car. Even though I couldn't quite make out how he looked, I did notice that Fatu was extremely dark-skinned, even darker than Bintu with a set of white teeth, so I smiled at him too and said hi. Then I turned back around in my seat so that Nikki could continue her conversation with Bintu.

Two minutes later, I nudged her in her arm, letting her know to wrap up her conversation because I was ready to go. Fortunately for me, she took heed and we were out of there before I could count to ten. She did exchange numbers with Bintu, and on the way home, Nikki filled my head up with everything she learned about the man.

"I'm definitely calling him," Nikki didn't hesitate to say. "Did you see his 2008 S-Class Benz he was driving?" she asked in amazement.

I chuckled. "Yes, Nikki, I did."

"Do you think it's paid for?"

"Probably not."

"Well, did you see his brother Fatu?"

"No, I couldn't see him."

"Too bad, because he was handsome as shit, and he had a nice body."

"Now how did you see all that while he was sitting in the car?"

"He got out of the car to put some garbage in the trash can while you were in the store."

"Well, if he was all that, then why didn't you talk to him?"

"You know what? I started to, but when I thought about it, I decided that my best bet would be to try to hook up with the driver, since he was more likely to be the one with the most money."

"That isn't always true," I interjected.

"Well, it doesn't matter because Bintu told me him and Fatu own a nightclub downtown."

"Oh really?" A light bulb went off in my head, and all I could see was dollar signs. "What else did he tell you?" I continued.

"Well, he told me a lot of stuff. But what stuck out more than anything was the fact that he said he was thirty-five. He's single, and he lives in an apartment not too far from his nightclub."

"Where is he from?"

"Nigeria." She smiled.

"I see you over there grinning. You like these Nigerian niggas running 'round here, huh?"

"They a'ight."

"Yeah, tell me anything. But, you better be careful because those men are very dominating and controlling. And not only that, their culture is different than ours. They believe in having three and four wives, and they treat them like second-class citizens."

"I know, I heard about that. But Bintu doesn't strike me as being that type."

"Don't let his look fool you."

"I'm not. But I am going to find out what he's working with so I can get him to spend some of that money he got on me."

I laughed. "Getcha own damn money, will ya?"

"Oh, I am. But I want to get in his pockets too."

"What if he's the stingy type?"

"Then I'ma cut off his ass."

"Well, please don't give him any coochie until he invests some major dough in it."

"Come on, Kira, you know I'm hip to the game. And I'ma prove it to you, because he invited us to come to his white party at his nightclub tomorrow night, and we're going."

"How you gon' tell me where I'm going tomorrow night?" I asked. "And you know I don't do the nightclub scene anyway."

"Yeah, I know. But what else we got to do? We don't do shit but get up every morning, go to work, and come back home."

"Nikki, what are you talking about? We go places."

"Kira, the only places we ever go are to the mall and out to eat. That's it. And I'm tired of doing the same ol' things. I want to get out and do more things. Meet more people. I mean, look at us, we are some pretty-ass women, and we are not getting any younger. So instead of letting the grass grow underneath our feet, we need to get out and see the world."

"I am fine living my life the way it is right now."

"Come on now, Kira! We've been in Houston for almost four months now, and we haven't done anything new and exciting."

"Believe me, we done enough exciting shit back in Virginia to last us a lifetime," I replied sarcastically.

"You need to lighten up and go out with me just this one time," she begged.

"I don't know, Nikki."

"Come on, Kira, it's just a white party. And besides, Bintu said that the only people who are coming are the ones he invited."

Not at all moved by the excitement in Nikki's voice, I shook my head with uncertainty. "I still don't know," I said, because in all actuality I wasn't in the mood to be around a whole lot of people I didn't know. I was still dealing with the issues I left back in Virginia, which were going to take me some time to get over. In addition, I didn't know how these guys were. For all we knew, they could be a couple of psychos. And since I'd exhausted all my energy from dealing with those types of niggas in my past, I refused to entertain another one at this time in my life. Now don't get me wrong, I still craved the idea of being one with a man who respected and loved me, but the way my luck was, it seemed that there wasn't a man out there who fit that bill. So in the meantime, I would just lay low and keep my eyes opened.

"All right, I'll tell you what," Nikki continued. "Let's just go out and check out the atmosphere of the party. If you don't like the vibe, then we can leave right back out. But if you feel comfortable, then we can stay as long as you like. It's your call."

I hesitated for a moment and then said, "What time does it start?"

"It's from ten to three."

"All right. I'll go this time, but if we go there and these people make me feel out of place, or start playing that whack-ass African drumbeat music and all the women start dancing in the middle of the floor like they're performing an African ritual, I am going to get right up and leave."

Nikki burst into laughter. "I don't think it's going to be that type of party."

"I hope not." I pulled into the driveway of my home.

Once we were inside, I settled down on the living room sofa and watched *American Idol*. Nikki took her food into the kitchen so she wouldn't disturb me while she was talking to her new friend Bintu on her Blackberry. I told her not to call him until tomorrow, so it wouldn't seem like she was sweating him, but she wouldn't listen. I threw up my hands and said, "Whatever!"

Taking My Best Shot
(Nikki Speaks)

I could tell Kira was hating on me for leaving her silly ass in the living room while I took my food and my conversation to the kitchen. Shit, I was trying to get to know my new friend without any distractions. I picked at my food and had myself a nice little chat with Bintu. His accent was really cute. What was even more appealing about him was that he was a business owner with a ninety-thousand-dollar whip, so I knew he was caked up with a lot of dough. I couldn't wait to get my hands on some of it. I was well aware that in order for me to tap into his pockets I was going to have to play my cards right, and that was what I intended to do.

"So how long have you been living in Houston?" I asked him.

"Five years now."

"How long have you been in America?"

"Since I was nineteen."

"Well, what made you want to come here, if you don't mind me asking?"

"My parents sent me here to further my education, so I went to Columbia University in New York, and after I graduated with a bachelor's degree in civil engineering, I worked for my uncle in his restaurant for three years so I could save enough money to open my own business. Once I accomplished that, I followed my brother out here to Houston, and we got the ball rolling."

"What's the name of your nightclub?"

"Club Reign."

"How is business?"

"Business is very good. Our fifth-year anniversary is tomorrow, so that's why we're having the white party."

"Oh, OK."

"Have you decided if you and your cousin are coming?"

"Yeah, we're coming."

"Good. I'm glad, because you and your cousin are going to be my special guests. I'm going to make sure you two are treated like queens!"

"Aww, Bintu, that's so nice! But I am not trying to get into any drama when your wife sees you catering to me and my cousin."

"I already told you that I don't have a wife."

"Well, I know you've got to be seeing somebody."

"No, I'm not seeing anyone right now," he replied.

"Well, have you ever been married?"

"No."

"When was the last time you were in a relationship?"

Bintu hesitated for a moment, then sighed heavily. "Well, let me see," he began. "My last relationship was about six months ago, and we were together for about two years."

"Why did y'all break up?"

"Because we figured out that we didn't want the same things."

"What kind of things are you talking about?"

"Well, for one, she didn't want to have children, and I did. We used to always argue back and forth when that issue came up, and I got sick of it."

"How many children do you want to have?"

"Three or four."

"Well, don't you want to get married first?"

"In my country, it is forbidden for a man and woman to have children out of wedlock, so I would definitely marry the woman first."

"Well, have you ever thought about moving back to Nigeria?"

"Oh, yes, I have," he responded with excitement. "I plan to go back home right after I make a couple million dollars, so I can build a small castle for me and my family."

"Who? Your wife and kids?"

"Yes, of course, but I was also talking about my parents."

Hearing this nigga tell me he was going to build a house so his parents could live with him gave me a really bad taste in my mouth. Was he fucking kidding me? Who did that bullshit? If I ever married a man and he told me he was building a house big enough so that his parents could live with us, I would ask him for the divorce papers because there wasn't no way in the world that shit was going to work. Thank God I wasn't trying to be with this cat for the long haul, because if I was, I would be up shit's creek without a paddle!

I changed the subject. "Do you do anything else other than run the club?"

"I've got a few other investments, but they're minor." He changed the subject this time. "What about you?"

"What about me?" I replied.

"What do you do?"

"Well, I'm co-owner of a hair salon in the uptown district. Now, it may not gross a lot of revenue like your nightclub, but it damn sure pays the bills."

"What's the name of your salon?"

"It's called Creative Images."

"In what part of the district is it located?"

"It's on Monroe Street, near the Greyhound bus station."

"I know where that is. Do you do hair yourself?"

"Sometimes I'll wash a couple of the stylists' client's hair or prep them for a relaxer or what have you, but normally I handle the receipts and the paperwork for the day-to-day operations."

"What about your cousin? Does she do hair?"

"Yep, she sure does. As a matter-of-fact, she's the other owner."

"Is she married?"

Shocked by his question, I hesitated for a bit and then answered, "No. Why?"

"Because my brother Fatu is very fond of her. He talked about how beautiful she was all the way to the nightclub."

"Well, I'll make sure I tell her that after I get off the phone with you." I had no intention whatsoever of telling Kira that she had been the main subject of the brothers' conversation. I mean, why should I? All it was going to do was go to her head. Besides, I was tired of standing in her shadow! I was much prettier than she was, and if they couldn't see that, then something was definitely wrong with their eyes. Not only that, I had my eyes on Fatu first, so why was he sweating Kira? She wouldn't give him the time of day, which was another reason why I wouldn't waste my time telling her. Fatu was not her type, so to hell with them both.

Our conversation lasted another ten minutes and then we called it a night. I did assure Bintu that Kira and I were still coming to his party, and that we would call him before we headed his way.

Kira was still sitting on the sofa, watching TV, when I walked back into the living room. I cracked a smile at her the moment she looked up at me. "I heard you in there, giggling," she teased. "What, you in love?"

"Hell nah!"

"Well, something is going on, because you are smiling your ass off!"

"All I was doing was trying to get to know the cat." I took a seat next to her.

"What was he talking about?" I gave her a recap of my conversation with Bintu. When I told her about his plans to build himself a big enough house so that his parents could live there as well, Kira burst into laughter. "So, when is the wedding?"

Shocked by Kira's response, I laughed too. "Girl, please! That'll never happen. But I don't mind playing like we're married until I can suck every dime he owns out of him."

"All that sounds good, but you better be careful, because African men aren't stupid. Whatever kind of scheme you got cooking up, know that you've got to go at it hard, or don't go at it at all."

"Trust me, I've got it under control."

"I hope so, because cats like your friend Bintu are of a different breed. Believe me, he ain't like them other cats we've dealt with. You know all those other niggas we fucked with wasn't concerned about if we were with them for their dough, because they had their own agenda. But Bintu seems like the type of cat who'd go upside your head if he had the slightest clue that you only wanted him for his money."

"Girl, please! I wish that nigga would put his hands on me."

"Don't think it won't happen because he was smiling all up in your face tonight and saying all the right things. Give him a couple of months and watch how his true colors come out."

"Come on, now, you know I know what time it is. That's why I'm going to play my cards right."

"Yeah, you better," Kira warned. "Because you've got to remember that we're way out here all by ourselves, and I ain't gon' be able to take on your man and his peoples all by myself. So give him a little bit of coochie, suck his dick a few times, and get whatcha can, but don't be greedy."

"I won't," I assured her, knowing I was going to get everything I could. On some low shit, I do listen and take some of Kira's advice, but I have come to the realization that if I continue to do just that, I am going to always stay in her shadow and never be on her level and I am tired of that shit. So, from that day forward, I was going to do what the fuck I felt was best for me. And if I wanted to get a little bit of dough from Bintu's ass and fuck him on a regular, then that's what I would do. Contrary to popular belief, giving a cat some pussy for some monetary gain hasn't ever hurt me; that's why I fucked around with Sophie's ugly-ass husband. He wasn't really working with much because he had three wives to take care of, but he did his part when it came to me. I never told Kira how he took me on an overnight excursion to a nice hotel on the Westside and then took me shopping and spent about six hundred dollars on me. I mean, it wasn't much, but hey, at least he didn't make me feel like a cheap trick. And besides, it ain't like I was trying to marry the cat anyway. All I wanted to do was get my nut off and see what I could get out of him. That was it. Now I was on some new shit. And since Bintu was next on my list, I was going to see what I could get out of his ass too. Whether it would be an ass whooping or a trunk filled with dough, I was going to test the waters.

Special Delivery

(Kira Speaks)

The next day Nikki told me she was going to drive her own car to work because she had some errands she needed to run, so I went ahead and left without her. Once I got to the shop and opened the doors, all my stylists came falling in, one behind the other, and got right to work. Everything was running smoothly. It was peaceful, and I loved it. But whoever said that all good things came to an end was right, because it wasn't long before Nikki came waltzing through the front door of the shop with a handful of shopping bags, bragging about how good she was going to look at the white party.

"Y'all ain't gon' believe all the hot shit I picked up at the mall this morning," she crowed.

"Where did you go?" Carmen asked.

Carmen was the diva around here. She resembled the singer Ciara, but with a little more weight. Niggas loved her, and she'd tell you quick that she only fucked with the ones who had plenty of dough to spend on her. Just a couple of months ago, though, she decided to settle down with this well-known cat named Xavier. People in the streets called him X. From what I heard, he ran the entire Irvington Village projects down on Fulton Street, so he got a lot of paper, and with paper came respect.

In a small way, X kind of reminded me of Ricky. He didn't physically resemble him at all, but you could tell that X's fat ass was very cocky and he was definitely a ladies' man. Carmen could care less about the other women, though. She'd tell you quick that she was known as his main chick, and all the bitches in the streets knew it, so that was all that mattered. She was also known around Houston for nine-hundred-dollar lace-front wigs, so she kept a nice piece of change in her pockets, along with the latest eleven-hundred-dollar handbag thrown over her shoulder. I knew she had to have every designer handbag and shoe that Neiman Marcus and Saks Fifth Avenue ever sold. She could tell if a chick was carrying a knock-off bag from a mile away.

"I went up to Post Oak Boulevard and ran into Galleria Mall and had myself a ball," Nikki replied as she tossed her bags on top of her station.

"What did you get?" Carmen asked.

"Yeah, what kind of hot shit you supposedly just bought?" I added while I worked a perm into my client's hair.

Nikki picked up a Neiman Marcus bag and pulled out a seven-hundred-dollar sleeveless white MaxMara asymmetrical strap blouse and a four-hundred-twenty-dollar white fitted pencil skirt by Christian Dior. "What y'all think?" she asked as she held both pieces of clothing next to her body.

"I like it," I commented.

"Yeah, that shit is hot!" Carmen interjected.

I continued to stare at the outfit. "What kind of shoes are you wearing?"

Nikki replaced her top and skirt back into the bag and removed a shoebox from another Neiman Marcus bag. "I'm going to wear these." She removed the lid and pulled out a pair of three-inch, silver, Christian Dior T-strap sandals.

"Damn! Those sandals are vicious as hell! How much did you pay for them?" Carmen practically drooled over the shoes.

"Yeah, how much were they?" I wanted to know.

"Six hundred," Nikki replied proudly.

Not knowing how to respond, I just stood there with a look of uncertainty on my face. Nikki said, "Why are you looking like that?" Her tone was defensive.

"I'm just trying to figure out why you went out and spent all that money for some stuff you're only going to wear one time?"

"Simply because I wanted to, so I did it," Nikki snapped.

I tried to remain calm in the face of Nikki's stupidity. "OK, and that's fine. But don't you think you probably went just a little overboard?" I tried to get her to see it my way, because that couple hundred grand she snatched up before we left VA was bound to be gone any day if she kept throwing it away on shit like that.

Nikki immediately took offense and abruptly stuffed her shoes back into their box. "Do I say that to you when you go into Saks and drop twenty-two hundred on a Chloe bag, or fifteen hundred on a Marc Jacobs dress?"

"No, you don't. And that's only because you know I can afford to do that."

"So, you're saying I can't?" Nikki was visibly upset. The other stylists and clients in the salon were silent as they watched our argument with avid interest.

"No, I'm not saying that." I tried to answer in a way that would prevent an argument from starting, but it didn't work.

"So, what are you saying then?" Nikki threw the shoebox back into the shopping bag. "Because it sounds to me like you can't stand to see me have anything."

I felt my headache start to return. "Come on, now, Nikki! You are really blowing this out of proportion. And right now is not the time for it, especially around the customers. Can we drop it, please?" I returned my attention back to my client's hair.

"Yeah, you would want to drop it right after you get the last word." Nikki snatched her bags from her station and took them back into the office.

I ignored her childish behavior and let her carry her ass so I could continue servicing my client. I was definitely going to have a talk with her later about her behavior. I mean, how dare she attempt to suggest that I didn't want to see her with anything, like I was hating on her or something! Was she kidding me? I could clearly dance circles around her with the money and the wardrobe I had. I was the original trendsetter. Nikki didn't know a thing about wearing Gucci handbags with the shoes to match, nor had she ever worn a ten-thousand-dollar mink coat until she borrowed mine. She'd better get her act together before I pulled her coat and brought her ass back down to reality.

Several hours passed and Nikki limited her conversation with me as much as possible. The only time she said something to me was when I had a phone call on the salon phone, or if she needed to make change for my clients, and I was fine with that. She had a lot of conversation for Carmen and Rachael, my other stylist, though.

Rachael was the youngest of us all, and she sure knew how to run her mouth. She was married, and was a fair-looking girl in her early twenties who loved to wear her hair in microbraids. She kind of favored the R&B singer Brandy, but if you told her to sing something, she wouldn't be able to carry a note to the front door. If you ever wanted to know about anybody's business, nine times out of ten, Rachael had the scoop. That was why when she asked me questions about my personal life back in VA, I shut down her nosey ass. I simply told her that the life I lived back in Virginia wasn't any of her business. "Oh, my bad! I apologize," she said. But I told her that there was no need for an apology, because now she knew where I stood when it came to my personal life, so we shouldn't have that problem again. So far we hadn't.

I couldn't say the same for Nikki, because Rachael kept Nikki running her mouth about her business. Even though seventy percent of what Nikki told her was a lie, the fact remained that Nikki entertained Rachael's nosiness, and when Nikki least expected it, those very same lies were going to come right back and blow up in her face. I couldn't wait for that day, because when it came, I was going to laugh my ass off.

Meanwhile, we got a surprise visit from a short, white, middle-aged woman carrying a clipboard and a dozen red roses in a crystal vase. "May I help you?" I asked her.

"I have a delivery for Kira," she replied.

Shocked by this unexpected delivery, I stepped forward and said, "That's me." I was racking my brain trying to figure out who the hell could have sent me flowers. I hadn't been on a date since I'd been in Houston, and I hadn't met anyone, so who were these flowers from? I cradled the flowers in my left arm while I signed the delivery form, thanked the woman, and tipped her ten bucks before she made her exit. Immediately after she left I rushed back to my station, set down the vase, and grabbed the little pink-and-white card from the plastic guard.

"I wonder who sent me these flowers?" I asked aloud.

"Stop fronting, Kira. You know who sent them," Rachael interjected.

While I attempted to open the card, I smiled bashfully. "I swear, I do not know who sent this." My eyes nearly popped out of my head when I read the card.

Rachael and Carmen both rushed to my side. "Who sent it?" they both wanted to know.

Nikki didn't utter one word. She sat in her chair with her arms folded, I guess waiting for me to unveil the mystery of who sent me the roses. I looked at Rachael and Carmen and said, "Fatu."

Nikki jumped straight out of her seat. "Fatu?" she repeated incredulously.

I smiled at her. "That's what the card said."

"Who is Fatu?" Carmen asked.

"Yeah, who is he?" Rachael chimed in.

Before I could answer them, Nikki rushed over and grabbed the card out of my hands. "He's the brother of this guy I met last night," she blurted out. Her attitude was back in effect. After she read the card, she placed it on my station instead of putting it back into my hands.

"Oh shit! Kira's got a new man," Carmen teased.

"No, I do not," I protested.

"Well, tell us how he looks," Rachael suggested.

I shrugged. "I can't really tell you because it was dark. Plus, he was sitting in the car when Nikki's friend introduced him to me."

"Well, did y'all get to talk?" Rachael pestered.

"No. All I did was say hi."

Carmen put her hands on her hips and said, "You mean to tell us that all you did was said hi to this cat, and he went out and had a dozen red roses delivered to you?"

I nodded. It may have sounded strange, but it was true.

Carmen shook her head. "Well, that's kind of hard to believe."

"Ask Nikki. She was there."

Carmen and Rachael turned to Nikki, who had returned to her chair. "Is she telling the truth or what?" Rachael asked.

Nikki sighed heavily, as if she really didn't want to be bothered. She reluctantly said, "She ain't lying."

Satisfied, Rachael directed more questions at me. "Well, did he write anything in the card besides his name?"

"Yes." I smiled.

"Well, what did he say?"

"Yeah, tell us what it said," Carmen added.

I blushed. "All he said was that I was beautiful, and he hoped that I enjoyed the roses."

"Did he put his number in there?" Carmen pressed.

"Nope."

"So how are you going to call and thank him?"

"Yeah, that would be nice," Rachael added.

"The only way I would be able to get in contact with him is if Nikki called his brother."

Rachael and Carmen both turned and looked at Nikki.

Nikki snapped, "What y'all looking over here for?"

"Girl, don't play stupid!" Rachael replied. "Pull out that Blackberry and call your friend, so Kira can thank his brother for the roses."

Judging by Nikki's expression, she looked like she wanted to tell both of them to mind their business for once, but thank God she decided to hold her tongue, because I wasn't in the mood to hear another negative word come out of her mouth. I was sure that everyone else, including the clients, felt the same way. When Nikki retrieved her phone from her handbag, Rachael, Carmen, and I stood there in amazement as Nikki mustered up a fake smile and made the call to Bintu.

"Hi, Bintu, this is Nikki. Are you busy?" she asked him. He must've said no and asked her what was up, because she immediately went into a spiel about my special delivery from Fatu, and that the only reason she was making this call was because I wanted to thank him. A few seconds later, Nikki looked at me and said, "Write down this number."

I found an ink pen inside my appointment book. "Go 'head."

"It's 713-555-1021."

After that she turned her chair around for privacy and continued to chat with Bintu. I noticed her voice changed to a sexy tone, and then she giggled like she was just the sweetest thing in the world. I had to hand it to her, she sounded like she could work for a phone sex company. I couldn't make out what she was saying, and I really didn't care, so I used the shop's phone to dial the number Nikki had just given me. Surprisingly, my heart started beating faster. I didn't understand why, because it wasn't like I was nervous about speaking to this guy. I mean, I didn't have anything to prove to him. I took a deep breath and listened to the phone ring. After three rings, he finally answered.

"Hello, am I speaking with Fatu?" I asked while Carmen and Rachael practically stared down my throat.

"Yes, you are," he replied.

"Well, I'm Kira. The one you sent the roses to. I just called to say thank you."

"Oh, you are so very welcome! And I hope you enjoy them."

"I will."

"Are you coming to our white party tonight?"

"Well, I plan to if I can get out of here on time."

"Well, please do, because I would love to see your beautiful face again."

I blushed again. "That's sweet of you to say."

"No, I'm serious. You are a very beautiful woman. I talked about you all the way to the nightclub last night. And when Bintu came into my office and told me that you weren't married, I got really excited and thought it would be a good idea to make a more formal introduction of myself by sending you the flowers."

"Do you send roses to every beautiful woman you run into?"

"Oh no! Of course not! I see beautiful women all the time, but there was just something about you that stuck out more so than the rest of them."

"I'm sure," I commented.

"So, is there anything I can say or do to make sure you come out tonight?"

"No. You don't have to do anything," I assured him.

"Does that mean you're coming?"

I hesitated for a few seconds because I didn't want to give him the impression that I was pressed to come out to his function. "What time does this party start?"

"Nine."

"Well, I might be a little late, because my last client probably won't be leaving out of here until seven-thirty. And then on top of that, I'm gonna have to go by the mall to find something white, and that'll probably take me about an hour or so to do. And then I'm going to have to run home to take a shower so I can change, and then I'll be able to head your way."

"Can I make a suggestion?" Fatu asked.

"Sure."

"Would you mind if I sent my personal shopper over to your place of business, so you wouldn't have to make that extra trip out to the mall?"

I knew I didn't hear him right. "Your what?"

"My personal shopper," Fatu repeated.

"And what would this person do?"

"There's a woman my brother and I use to do our personal shopping for us. She works for Saks Fifth Avenue. If you're up for it, I can have her come to you with a large selection of clothing, and that way, you wouldn't have to go out."

Shocked by his generous gesture, I asked him how much this

service would cost.

"Not to worry! My brother and I spend an awful lot of money there, so they would do this small favor as a courtesy. Tell me, who are your two favorite designers?"

Oh, my God! Was this nigga serious? Was he really going to send his personal shopper to my shop with a shitload of clothes so I could pick out something to wear that night? I mean, damn! I had plenty of cats take me to Bergdorf Goodman, as well as all the other expensive-ass stores to spend a lot of dough on me, but I never had one of them call a store and have one of the store's representatives bring their merchandise to me. Today I was going to find out how that felt.

After I thought for a few moments, I lied and told Fatu that Vera Wang and Heidi Weisel were my favorite designers. I hadn't ever owned a thing from either of them. Prada, Dior, Gucci, and Roberto Cavalli were my favorite designers, and I had a closet full of clothes to prove it. Now that I was about to add Vera and/or Heidi to my collection, I was going to be one bad bitch for real!

Fatu and I ended our conversation shortly after I gave him my dress and shoe sizes. I made sure to tell him how thankful I was that he'd go through so much trouble to make sure I had something to wear that night.

"Believe me, it's no problem," Fatu assured me before we said goodbye. I had literally just hung up the telephone when Carmen damn near jumped into my arms.

"Did I just hear you give this man your dress and shoe sizes?" Her eyes were filled with excitement.

I smiled and nodded.

"Don't smile. Spill the beans! Tell us what's going on," Carmen insisted.

"Yeah, tell us what he said," Rachael added.

I sat in my chair and looked over to see what Nikki was doing. She was still on the phone with Bintu. I huddled the girls in closer and spoke in a low whisper. "When I told him that I was going to be late to his party because I still hadn't had a chance to go out and buy something white, he insisted that I let him send a personal shopper from Saks over here with a couple of racks of clothes so I could do my shopping while I'm working."

"You have got to be kidding me!" Rachael exclaimed. "You mean to tell me that this man is getting someone from Saks to come all the way over here with some clothes so you can pick out something to wear tonight?"

"Yep," I said proudly.

"Now, that's some fly shit!" Rachael nodded in approval.

"You sure ain't lying about that," Carmen commented. "Because I didn't know that stores like that would send their merchandise out so that regular customers could shop away from the store. I knew they did it for celebrities, or people who got plenty of money."

"Well, I guess Fatu is one of those people with plenty of money," Rachael concluded with a smile.

"Yeah, it seems that way," I agreed.

"It sure does. But what I want to know is, what time can we expect the clothes to get here? I'm dying to see what kind of stuff he's going to send." Carmen looked at her watch with impatience.

"I can't wait to see what comes through that door, either."

I sat back and imagined how everything was going to go down when the personal shopper came strolling through the door. I also envisioned how Nikki was going to react. She had already started hating when she found out that Fatu had the roses delivered to me, so I knew she was going to be devastated when she saw that he'd spent some serious dough to get a personal shopper from Saks to bring me something to wear to his party. What was really going to be special was Nikki's facial expression while I went through a rack of designer clothing right here at my place of business, courtesy of my new friend Fatu. She was going to be hating her ass off, and I was going to love every minute of it.

I continued to service my clients while I waited for my clothes to arrive. It didn't seem like I had to wait that long because after I got the next two clients out of my chair, I received a call from a young woman named Ashley, telling me that she was outside the shop with a service van filled with Saks merchandise, but she had nowhere to park. I told her I would be out in a minute to assist her. I grabbed my car keys from my handbag and asked Rachael to run outside with me, since Carmen was busy doing a sew-in for one of her clients. Nikki was still sitting in her chair, this time going over some receipts, so I left her right where she was.

When Rachael and I got outside we saw a white commercial van doubled-parked beside my car, which was parked directly in front of the shop. I walked up to the van and introduced myself to the driver, and told her that I was going to move my car around the corner so she could take my spot. Rachael would help her carry all the merchandise into the salon.

"Oh, thank you!" the woman said in relief. I pulled out of the parking space and let her pull into it.

After driving around the block twice, I finally found a parking space. Even though it was one-third of a mile from the shop, I didn't care, because I figured that what I was about to experience was going to be well worth the walk. And guess what? It truly was. That young white girl had my shop laid out with shit. She had three racks of clothes placed in the center of my lounge area. All the clothing items were white, neatly pressed, and hung on wooden hangers. I watched in amazement as Ashley sorted every single piece, including a dozen boxes of shoes. I could see all of the name brands of the shoes she brought out for me to choose from. The red Jimmy Choo box stuck out like a sore thumb, so I especially wanted to see those first.

While I waited for Ashley to take the plastic protectors off all the clothes, I saw Nikki through my peripheral vision gritting on me really hard. She was literally staring at me like she hated my fucking guts, so I casually turned my head in her direction, and as soon as my eyes landed on her, she quickly stood and rushed off toward the restroom as if she was in desperate need of a bathroom break. I laughed to myself and shook my head because she was really pathetic. Like I said before, if she didn't straighten out her attitude, shit was going to really get ugly between us, and I was going to come out on the winning end. You could bet your last dollar on that.

"Are you ready?" Ashley asked. Her smile showed off her deep dimples and a perfect set of white teeth.

"Yes, I am." I smiled. "You have such a beautiful smile."

"Thank you," she replied bashfully and proceeded to unveil her entire collection. Everything she brought with her had price tags of at least twenty-five hundred dollars. I honestly didn't know what the hell to choose because everything she had was so nice.

"Can I ask you a question?" I asked.

"Sure."

"Did Fatu give you any instructions about how much money I could spend?"

Ashley shook her head. "No, he didn't."

"Well, did he give me a limit on the things I could choose? Because from where I'm standing, I'm not in a good position right now."

"What do you mean?"

"Ashley, you brought a lot of nice things in here, and I'm finding it very hard to choose what I like the best."

Ashley giggled. "Trust me, you're not alone. I make these trips every day, and all of our clients say the same thing. But if it's any consolation, Mr. Oduka told me to let you have anything you want."

"Oh really?" Images of dollars signs floated around in my head.

"Yes, he did," Ashley assured me.

"OK, well let me ask you this. Has he ever had you to shop for other women?"

"I'm not at liberty to say. But just know that he's a very generous man." She winked.

Taking heed of that little bit of information, I smiled and convinced myself that money was no object for Fatu, and that I might as well have me a good ol' time. I tried on everything I thought would look nice. Carmen and Rachael cheered me on from the sidelines. Nikki, on the other hand, sat back in silence and watched me parade around in every Vera Wang and Heidi Weisel item that I grabbed off the rack. I wasn't going to let her get off that easy. I wanted to irritate the hell out of her, so I marched right over to her with my most sincere expression and asked, "Be honest. How does this dress look on me?"

Nikki looked at me from head to toe and said, "It's a'ight," with forced nonchalance.

"Tell me what you don't like about it." I pressed the issue because of the jealousy stamped across her entire face. It didn't matter that the dress was a thirty-seven-hundred-dollar Heidi Weisel strapless, silk, bustier dress, or that my 36-24-38 measurements complemented it perfectly. The only thing that struck a cord with Nikki was that I was the wrong person wearing it (meaning: not her), so she was definitely going to say something negative.

"Well, first off, it's too tight around your butt. So when you sit down, the threads might unravel."

"Come on now, Nikki, it ain't that tight," Carmen disagreed.

"It sure isn't," Rachael added.

Nikki frowned. "Yes, it is."

"Well, did you like that satin Vera Wang cami-style dress I just took off?" My questions continued, even though I knew she loathed the fact that I was getting the royal treatment.

"Nah, I really didn't like that one." She screwed her mouth up distastefully.

"Nikki, now you know that dress was nice as hell!" Rachael blurted out.

Nikki rolled her eyes. "Maybe it was nice to you, but I didn't like it."

"Well, I thought it looked really nice on her, if I may say so myself," Ashley interjected.

"I liked it too, and that would be the one I'd pick," Carmen added.

I thought for a moment and then asked Ashley, "Do you think Fatu would mind if I got the Vera Wang dress I just took off, and the satin-and-lace Heidi Weisel bustier with the coordinating pencil skirt?"

"I don't see why that would be a problem," she replied.

"Well, I guess that settles it."

"Have you decided on the shoes?"

"Yes. I definitely want those four-inch, cage-front Jimmy Choo sandals, and if you could throw in those three-and-a-half-inch, open-toed Bruno Frisoni ribbon sandals, that would be great."

"You got it."

As Ashley started packing up all of my new things, I slipped back into the office to change back into my own attire. When I returned to the lounge area with the Heidi Weisel silk bustier dress in my hand, I overheard Nikki asking Ashley what would it cost to buy the same items I just picked. Ashley told her that it would cost in the ballpark of about eleven thousand dollars. Nikki's eyes got bigger than fifty-cent coins. "Are you serious?" she asked.

Ashley nodded.

"Well, what would it cost me if I wanted you to do a little shopping for me, and then bring the things by my house?"

"Well, you would either have to have an account with us, or be a preferred customer who spends at least one hundred thousand dollars a month, whether it's in our Saks store or online. Once that's established, all you would need to do is get in touch with our Concierge Service, and we would handle it from there."

"Wow! Thanks!" I could see Nikki's mind racing with possibilities. She was probably trying to figure out how to get Bintu to hook her up at Saks.

"You're quite welcome." Ashley continued to pack up.

I refused to allow this woman to be bombarded with any more of Nikki's questions.

"You can't forget this," I said, holding out the Heidi Weisel dress.

"Don't worry, I didn't forget it. But I'm sure Mr. Oduka would not have minded you getting this dress as well." She winked and took the dress out of my hands.

I stood there and wondered if I should've added that dress to my collection. Then I figured, why be greedy? The way shit was going, there were bound to be more opportunities like this one. I settled for what I already had and was very satisfied.

Before Ashley left the shop, I slipped her a one-hundred-dollar tip and thanked her for a wonderful experience. She shook my hand, handed me her business card in the event I might need her services in the near future, and left with her racks of clothes in tow, again carried by Rachael. I called Fatu to thank him again. He sounded like he was more excited than I was, so I played right along with him.

"Well, you know what this means, right?" I asked.

"No, tell me," he insisted.

"This means that I will definitely be showing up at your party on time."

"That really makes me happy."

"I'm glad."

"So, did you get everything you needed?"

"Oh, of course I did. Ashley was so nice and helpful."

"Good, I'm glad." Fatu sounded as if he'd just done a good deed. I massaged his ego a little, and I did it loud enough for Nikki to hear me. Surprisingly, she didn't feed into my antics this time. Instead, she got up from her chair and announced that she was going to make a run to Quiznos to get a sub, and to let her know if anyone else wanted anything. No one made any requests, so she left.

My conversation with Fatu only lasted another five minutes because he said he had to take another call. "Oh, OK. Take care of your business," I insisted.

"Can I call you back?"

"Sure."

"OK. I'll call back after I get off this conference call."

"All right," I said.

We hung up, and I waited for the return call I knew I would get.

Bumping Heads
(Nikki speaks)

I had to get the hell out of that shop before I said something I might regret later. I mean, come on, how thick did she want to pour it on? Granted, the nigga spent a few coins on her and copped her some Heidi Weisel and some Jimmy Choo sandals. So what? I had a nigga who'd do the same damn thing for me. Kira needed to stop acting like she was the only chick in the world with a man who had money. I saw that I'd have to be the bitch to show her, because as soon as I got Bintu the way I wanted him, I was going to have that nigga spending his money on me like his mind was going bad. What was going to really fuck up Kira's head was when he put me in a big-ass house after I gave him some of this good pussy I got. Trust me, I was going to blow that bitch's mind, and when I did, she was going to want to take a few lessons from me. That was a promise I intended to keep.

The moment I arrived at Quiznos, I ordered my usual chicken and Swiss Sammies with a large sweet ice tea. While I waited for my order, this five feet eleven, well-built pretty boy with long cornrows strolled inside the restaurant with a huge iced-out chain around his neck, Prada sunglasses, and an iPhone pasted to his ear. Trust me, that old R&B singer Christopher Williams didn't have shit on this cat, so he was eye candy for sure. I played it cool and acted as if I hadn't noticed him when he came through the door. I could tell by his swagger that he knew he looked good, so I flat out refused to feed his ego anymore.

Besides, I shouldn't have been all up in his face anyway. As good as I looked, he should've been staring at me the moment *he* walked through the door. I knew he was a little distracted by the conversation he was having on his cell phone, but I looked good, so he should have at least taken a quick look when he passed by me. I mean, damn! My ass was so phat, it stuck out like a sore thumb. Tell me how he missed that?

Well, whatever he had going on in his head, it wasn't normal. If he knew like I knew, he had better snap back into reality before I walked out of there, because I was a good catch. Besides, I would love to add his number to my collection. Shit, I'd been in Houston far too long not to be exclusive with one of the ballers around there. I had a lot to offer, and if someone would just step up to the plate and do what they were supposed to do, then I'd be able to show them what I could add to their life. Until then, I guessed I was going to be doing just what I was doing now—standing alone.

Pretty boy finally ended his call when he realized that the woman behind the counter wasn't going to take his order until he did so. There was a big-ass sign taped next to the register that said: No CELL PHONE USE AT THE REGISTER, but since he was so engrossed in his conversation, he didn't notice it.

"Can I get a twelve-inch steak and cheese sub with extra mushrooms and cheese?" he asked.

"Would you like to add a bag of chips and a drink for two dollars more?" the cashier asked.

"Yeah, go 'head." He paid her for his order, was handed his receipt, and told to wait at the other end of the counter because his order would be up shortly.

I stood there with my arms folded like my shit didn't stink as he walked toward me. The beautiful part about all of this was the fact that he noticed me this time. He sized me up to the tenth power and I saw it all through my peripheral vision. I was tickled pink and loved the attention, but I refused to turn around and acknowledge him. I figured since he was checking me out, then he'd make the first move. And guess what? I was right. Homeboy got within two feet of me and said, "I can't believe your man let you out of the house by yourself."

I slightly turned my head and said, "What if I told you to believe it?"

He smiled. "Then I would tell you to get rid of him, because he ain't the man for you."

"But what if I refuse to do that, because I feel like he is the man for me?"

"Then I would tell you to let me take you out so I can make you feel otherwise."

I chuckled a bit because this guy was funny as hell and very determined, which were good qualities to have when dealing with me.

"What's so funny?" he asked as he got a little closer to me.

I took two steps backward. "You're funny! And why you had to get so close? You were fine where you were at."

He cracked another smile. "Yeah, a'ight! I'ma let you slide with that. But you got to tell me your name."

"Ma'am, here's your order," the woman behind the counter said. I took my bag from her and when I stepped back, this guy was dead on me.

"I'm waiting," he reminded me.

"You tell me your name first," I demanded.

"My name is Neeko."

"Is Neeko your real name?"

"Nah, it's Nathan, but I prefer everybody to call me Neeko."

"Why? Nathan is a nice name."

"Yeah, it's a'ight. But I'm waiting on you to tell me your name."

"It's Nicole, but everyone calls me Nikki." I extended my hand for him to shake.

Neeko took my hand and shook it gently. "Nice to meet you, Nikki. Now, are you going to let me prove to you that I'm a better man than the one you got at home?"

"Do you think you'd be up for the challenge?"

"I think you need to be asking your man that."

"I will." I took a couple of steps to my right, indicating that I was ready to go.

"Whatcha in a rush for?"

"I got to get back to work."

"Where you work at?"

"Me and my cousin own a hair salon not too far from here."

"What's the name of it?"

"It's called Creative Images."

"A'ight. Well, can I have your number so I can call you later?"

"Sure. But don't let your girlfriend stumble across it, because I'm not into a whole lot of drama."

"My girl doesn't go through my stuff," he assured me. To hear him tell me that he had a girl kind of threw me for a loop. I was devastated, but at least he was honest. A lot of niggas lied right off the bat because all they wanted to do was get you somewhere alone so they could fuck you. For some reason, though, Neeko seemed like he wanted to keep it real with me, and the fact that he had another woman made him look that much more desirable. I knew that sounded sick, but it was the truth. I loved fucking with cats that had a significant other because it put me up to the challenge of trying to take him from her. I may not have come out on top every time, but I left with some very nice gifts.

What I intended to do with Neeko was just go with the flow and see what he was working with. I'd just met Bintu and we were in the process of trying to get to know each other, but at the end of the day, I was a single woman. I was young, sexy, and beautiful, and I didn't have time to be sitting around like I was some undesirable chick with low self-esteem. Shit! It was my time now and I was going to show all the bitches in Houston that if they didn't watch out, I was going to have their men.

Right after he and I exchanged numbers, he walked me out to my car and assured me that he'd call me later. I watched him as he walked to his car. It was very important that I saw what he drove because if it was something whack, then I was going to avoid his call when I saw his number come up. I was really critical about dealing with men with hoopties. I looked too good to be riding in one, especially since I was now pushing a 2008 Lexus LS 460. If a nigga couldn't come correct, then he didn't need to come at all.

Thank God, Neeko hopped into a new, pearl-white Yukon Denali truck. He had it sitting on 24-inch rims and the tires looked like they had just been sprayed with wet-look tire spray. They were shining like a big dawg, and I liked that. Then Neeko ruined the image when he pulled out of his parking space and turned his music up sky high, which was a complete turnoff. I hated when guys rode around with their music roaring through their car speakers. To me, it showed their immature side, so I guessed that was something that Neeko and I were going to have to work on.

Money Does Grow On Trees

(Kira Speaks)

I cannot tell you why Nikki proposed that we drive in separate cars to Bintu and Fatu's white party. We were going to the same venue, and since we lived together, we were going back to the same place when the night was over. *What is going on in her head?* I wondered. When I asked her, she told me the reason why she was driving her own car was because she wanted to ride alone and clear her head. That was a lie because earlier that day I overheard Nikki tell Carmen that she planned to drive her own car because she wanted Bintu to see it, so he'd know right off the bat that she was high maintenance, and if he really wanted to get with her, he'd have to come hard like Fatu. I started to intervene in her conversation, just to let her know that she shouldn't have to go the extra mile to prove anything to a man, but then I figured, why waste my breath? She wasn't going to listen to me anyway. I did what I do best and left well enough alone.

After I programmed Fatu's nightclub address into my GPS, it took me straight there while Nikki followed. The drive was approximately twenty-five minutes, and as soon as we got within one hundred yards of the club, we noticed that there was valet parking available. Nikki and I pulled up directly in front of the club and made use of it. One of the valet attendants handed me a ticket for my car and directed me to the VIP entrance. I tried to wait for Nikki so we could walk into the club together, but she was taking her precious time. I took one last look and made sure I was showing just enough cleavage in my Heidi Weisel bustier. The satin pencil skirt was working every curve I had. Once I felt like everything was in order, I put one Jimmy Choo sandal in front of the other and made my way inside.

It seemed like every eye in the entire place focused on me once I crossed the threshold. I immediately felt out of place because it seemed like I was the only American in the entire place. Although it was a white party, the women had on tailor-made, gold-and-white African garments with the head wraps to match. My own hair was tucked inside a lace-front wig cut into the style of a bob, not to mention the fact that my titties looked like they were about to spill over. I knew I was going to be the talk of the evening. I thanked God for Nikki because as soon as she walked in behind me with her tight-ass white Christian Dior pencil skirt and the complementary white asymmetrical blouse, she got just about as much eye service as I did.

"Why is everyone staring at us?" she yelled so I could hear her over the loud music.

"It's probably because we look good," I yelled back.

"And what kind of music are they listening to?"

"Beats me." I looked around the room to see if either Bintu or Fatu were in sight before I took another step inside.

"Are you looking for me?" I heard a voice yell from behind me. Nikki and I turned around and saw Bintu standing behind us with the biggest smile he could give. Nikki was very happy to see him.

"What kind of question is that? You know we were." She smiled and grabbed him by the arm, letting everybody in the place know that she was there especially for him. I saw a couple of women turn up their noses after Nikki embraced Bintu, and it was funny to see. After Nikki got her ten minutes of fame by throwing herself all over Bintu, we finally got a chance to speak to one another. He signaled one of his servers to bring Nikki and I each a glass of Cristal.

"Enjoy your champagne, and mingle with my other guests while I go get Fatu," he encouraged us. I wasn't about to go off and start introducing myself to a bunch of people I didn't know. Instead, Nikki and I headed over to the nearest table and sat down so that we could take a load off our feet. I wasn't going to lie. My shoes were fly as hell, but they were killing me. I guessed that was the price you had to pay to look gorgeous.

While the foreign-sounding music blared in our ears, I felt the need to spark up a conversation with Nikki. It would've looked really silly for us to be the only people sitting at the table, and we weren't talking to each other. I took another sip from my glass and said, "Are you glad you came out tonight?"

She hesitated for a moment, and then said, "Not really, because I thought it was going to be different than this. But, hey, we're here now, so I guess we're going to have to make the best of it."

"Yeah, I'm feeling you. I'm going to get me a couple more glasses of this Cristal, talk with Fatu a bit, and then I'm going to be on my way."

"Sounds like a plan to me," Nikki agreed.

"So, what do you think about Bintu?" I tried to get the conversation flowing.

"He's all right, I guess. Why do you ask?"

"Because I saw how happy you were to see him, that's all."

"Girl, please. I'm just trying to play the role so he can start piling off some of that dough he's got, and that's it."

I chuckled. Before I could come back with some advice, Bintu and Fatu popped up at our table.

"I found him," Bintu announced. When I saw that handsome, bald headed, six-feet-four, 215-pound man, I almost fainted. It was unbelievable. This man looked just like the model and actor Djimon Hounsou himself, and I wanted nothing else but to jump right into his fucking arms. I managed to hold my composure and gave him my prettiest smile as I extended my hand in greeting. "How are you?"

Fatu took my hand and kissed it. "I'm doing well, now that you're here."

My smile got bigger. "Likewise," I assured him.

He smiled right back and looked at Nikki, then asked her if she was enjoying herself. Of course she lied. Shit, I lied too when he asked me the same question. What were we supposed to do? Tell him that his party really sucked, and that we were ready to get out of there? No way! We had to be diplomatic about it, and it paid off.

A few moments later Fatu extended his hand and asked me to follow him. "I want you to meet someone." I took his hand and stood.

"Which way are we going?" I asked.

"On the other side of the room." He looked at me from head to toe. "Oh, by the way, you look stunning tonight!" He flashed me another smile, showing me his beautiful, white teeth.

"I have you to thank for that. But you look pleasing to the eye as well." I took one long look at the way his white linen shirt and pants fit his physique. I could tell the size of his dick from the first glance, and it was a sight to see. There was no question in my mind that it was at least eight or nine inches. Hopefully one day I'd get to try it out, because if it was anywhere near as good as it looked hidden beneath all that linen, then he and I were going to become very close.

"Thank you." He led me to a group of people huddled together, sipping on champagne while making small talk. It turned out that they were his immediate family members. He first introduced me to his mother and father. Mr. Oduka was a fairly decent-looking big guy. He reminded me of the actor James Earl Jones. Mrs. Oduka, on the other hand, wasn't all that attractive. I tried to come up with at least a dozen people to figure out who she reminded me of, and the only person I could think of was the late Florida Evans from *Good Times*. I couldn't tell if she had that same little Afro, since she too wore a head wrap, but she definitely resembled the late actress.

As I looked at them together, I couldn't imagine Mr. Oduka being faithful to her. I would bet my entire savings that he either had another wife, or he had a lot of women he tricked with back in Africa, because this lady didn't have a bit of sex appeal. I figured she had some self-esteem issues. The way that Mr. Oduka stared at me while she stood next to him led me to believe that she knew about his infidelity. Poor lady! The things we did to keep a marriage together because of money. And you know what? I wasn't mad at her. Shit, a girl had to do what a girl had to do.

Next up to bat was Fatu's sister, whom he called Suri. She was a bit on the chunky side, but she was fairly decent-looking in the face. I could tell that she bleached her skin a lot because she looked kind of flushed, and her face and neck skin tones didn't match. Other than that, she seemed like she was a pleasant person. I was also introduced to a couple of Fatu's male cousins, Kofi and Matthew, and they seemed a bit friendlier than the other family members. I could tell that they were much younger than Fatu and Bintu, but they had a swagger about them that would have you believe that they were also powerful men. When Fatu and I stepped away from his family, I asked him what Kofi and Matthew did for a living.

"They work for me," Fatu replied. "But they also have a couple small businesses on the side."

"Think I can get a job too?" I joked.

"You could work for me any day." Before I knew it, I had been escorted around the entire nightclub and was introduced to everyone but his servers. What was so interesting about my meeting everyone was that they wanted to know whether Fatu and I were a couple. He told a few of them that we were just friends, but the other ones, like his cousins and a few of the other men who were smiling all in my face, Fatu told them that I was his special lady, and I let him ride with that too. After all, he did earn that right after I ran up an eleven-thousand-dollar tab in his name. I just hoped that the spending didn't stop there.

Once Fatu made all his rounds, or rather showed me off to his people, we retired to his back office. I quickly took a seat on the black leather sofa and wasted no time removing my four-inch heels. When I started massaging my feet to soothe the aches, Fatu became a little concerned.

"Are you OK?" he asked.

I smiled. "I am fine, sweetie! I've just been standing on my feet too long, but I'll be all right."

"Let me help you with that," he said, grabbing my feet. But his plans were interrupted by a knock on the door.

He answered the door and Bintu walked in and handed him what appeared to be a small, brick-like object wrapped in newspaper. "This is from Ian," he stated.

"Is he outside?" Fatu wanted to know.

"No. He dropped off the money and left."

"OK. But let me know if Emmett comes, because I need to speak with him."

"No problem. I will be sure to let you know." Bintu turned around and made his exit.

After Bintu's departure, Fatu locked the door behind him. "I'm sorry for the interruption," he apologized.

"No need to apologize. Take care of your business," I encouraged him. Fatu unwrapped the package to reveal four ten-stacks of one-hundred-dollar bills, each with a ten-thousand-dollar bank label wrapped around it. He was holding forty thousand dollars in his hands. He placed the money inside a safe he had hidden in the wall, behind a mounted statue of an African goddess. I acted like I didn't see him put the money away because I didn't want to come across as being the nosey type.

Fatu returned and took a seat beside me on the sofa. We talked about everything under the sun. He told me he was thirty-six-years-old and Muslim, but he hadn't picked up his Koran in a while. He also said that his birthday was August 29, which meant that he was a Leo. His family was from Lagos, Nigeria, and they were very rich in their country. I was shocked as hell when he told me that shit. I had always believed that a lot of Africans grew up poor, which was why they came to America for a better life. I guess I learned my new thing for the day.

After he schooled me on his lifestyle back in Nigeria, he blew off my wig when he told me that his father had four wives, and that three of them lived back in Nigeria. I asked Fatu how many children his father had. When he told me that his father had eighteen children, I almost had a heart attack. I mean, there was not that much sex in the world. Not only that, I would not have allowed my man to marry another woman. I knew that was their culture over in Africa, so my best advice to them was that they needed to keep it over there, because I wasn't down with that bullshit. It was bad enough that I had to deal with Ricky cheating on me behind my back, but to know that I had to share my husband with a couple of bitches who'd probably live in the same house as me was unacceptable, and I would have let it be known.

Later in the conversation we talked about my likes, dislikes, and why I wasn't in a relationship. I briefly mentioned that I had been married before, but my husband was deceased. I didn't elaborate on the cause of his death, because I didn't want to scare Fatu away.

"How long has it been since he passed away?" Fatu asked with concern.

"It'll be two years next month."

"Has it been hard for you to move on with your life?"

"Let's just say that I moved out here to Houston specifically so that I could move on. There was no way I would have been able to move on from my past if I was still in Virginia. That place had nothing but bad memories for me, and I couldn't take it any longer."

"You must've been through a lot, because I see the hurt in your eyes."

"We'll just say that it was more than I could handle."

"Well, you're here now. And I'm going to make sure you're taken good care of."

"Fatu, you don't have to do that. Sweetie, you don't owe me anything."

"I know I don't. But I like you, and the people I like, I find myself making sure that they're all right."

"And that's fine. But you've done enough for me already."

"Come on, Kira! You can't be talking about today, because that was nothing."

Shocked by his words, I said, "Spending over eleven thousand dollars on me is nothing?"

"I'm talking for you. That amount of money is nothing compared to what you're worth."

I smiled and said, "I can't argue with you on that, Fatu. But that was still an awful lot of money to spend on someone you just met."

"Just imagine what I can do for you if we really knew each other," he said in his strong, manly voice. I had to admit that I was turned on.

There I was, sitting in the company of this tall, dark, sexy nightclub owner, who appeared to be swimming in dough. The good part about it was that he was single, hadn't ever been married, and didn't have any baby mamas. Now how sweet was that? More importantly, I could tell that Fatu was the boss of everybody, including Bintu. When Nikki found out that shit, she was going to have a fucking baby! But she'd be all right, because Bintu would take care of her, I was sure.

Fatu and I hung out with each other until a little after midnight. I had gotten tired, so I was ready to go home and hit the sack. He tried to convince me to stay a little longer, but I declined the offer.

"Well, can I take you out for breakfast in the morning?"

"I'm afraid I'm going to have to take a rain check on that, because I have a few clients coming in bright and early."

"Well, what about lunch?"

"What time are you talking about?"

"Maybe noon, or one o'clock."

"I'll let you know." I got up to leave.

He walked me back through the club so I could let Nikki know that I was about to leave. When I got halfway across the dance floor I noticed her at the bar in a deep conversation with Bintu. I told her I was about to leave, and she acted as if she didn't care. I wished her a safe drive home and left.

Outside the nightclub I gave Fatu a warm hug and kissed him on the cheek, thanking him once again for everything. He returned my kiss—a wet one, smack dab in the middle of my forehead—and told me to call him as soon as I reached home.

Welcome to America

(Nikki Speaks)

Kira must've been crazy if she thought I was going to leave with her while I was in the middle of a deep conversation. Shit, I was trying to get in good with this guy, and she was trying to fuck it up. She fucked up my relationship with Syncere because she couldn't keep her damn mouth closed, but I'd be damned if I let her come between this one. It wasn't going to happen. After her hating ass left, Bintu and I called it a night. He invited me to go back to his place, and I jumped at the opportunity. If Kira was around she'd try to talk me out of going, but I was a grown-ass woman. If I chose to spend the night at this man's house and let him fuck my brains out, then so be it. I could take care of myself and I was going to make sure that she saw that.

Before we left the club, Bintu had a few things he needed to take care of, so I went outside and waited in my car. It took him about fifteen minutes to bring his ass outside. He and another guy stumbled out the side door of the nightclub, dragging a third guy by his neck. My heart stopped. I couldn't believe what I was witnessing. Bintu slapped the third man around while his partner held him. "Don't ever let that shit happen again! You understand me?" I heard him say.

The slapped guy nodded. Before they let him walk off, Bintu

slapped him around a few more times and then took his wallet. The guy looked pitiful and I was starting to feel sorry for him. It became apparent that he had owed Bintu some dough and probably took a long time to pay him back, so my sympathy quickly wore off and I started cheering Bintu on inside my mind, thinking, *Yeah baby, don't let that nigga take advantage of you. Set that nigga straight!* I caught myself making hand movements too, like I was the one doing the slapping. Finally Bintu let the guy go, excused his partner, and brushed off his clothing before walking over to my car. He smiled at me like nothing happened. I played it off and smiled back.

"Ready?" I asked.

"Yes, I'm ready." He looked at my car strangely. "Wasn't this car red last night?" he asked.

"That was Kira's car. We got the same car. They're just different colors."

"Nice. Are you ready?"

"Yes, I am."

"Well, follow me." I waited for him to pull off in his Benz, then I followed.

The drive to Bintu's place only took us ten minutes. I was glad that we didn't have to drive very far. I smiled even more when I looked up and saw that we were in line for valet parking at the Uptown Galleria building. That building was filled with luxury apartments on every floor, and from what I'd heard, they cost a minimum of $1.5 million. If Bintu owned one of those apartments in that building, then he was richer than I'd thought.

As soon as we entered the building, we took the elevator to the top floor, which was the penthouse suite. When the elevator doors opened, my eyes nearly popped out of my head. The smoke gray, marble floors that led to Bintu's apartment door were immaculate and beautiful, but the artwork on the walls looked like something you'd see in a magazine. There was no doubt in my mind that they were very expensive pieces. I noticed a mini-video camera positioned right over the entryway of the apartment door, and I knew that Bintu had this floor on lock.

He unlocked the door with his keycard. "After you," he said, and followed me into the apartment. "Give me one second and I'll be with you." He walked over to the alarm control panel on the wall and keyed in his code to disarm the system. He turned on the lights and escorted me through the foyer to the living room area, which was huge with tall windows that gave a spectacular view of the water wall, Greenway Plaza, and the entire downtown area of Houston. "Have a seat and I'll be right back." He left the room.

I sat down on this beautiful black microfiber sofa that had a multicolored African throw draped across the middle of it, and took a glance around the entire place. The apartment was on two levels and arranged in a circular shape. All of the floors were beige marble trimmed in gold. I could also see the loft and the spiral staircase that led to it. In the loft area there was a library overlooking the living room. There were also four steel beams holding up the landing for the second floor, with a fireplace built into the walls of both floors, which I thought was really hot. What really topped off the whole place was the kitchen area. It was gorgeous with granite countertops, a breakfast bar, and the same gold-trimmed beige marble floors. Old-fashioned pots and pans hung from an iron rack that was suspended from the ceiling, right over the island. That was really nice. The faucet set in gold was something I thought I would never see inside a bachelor's house. It spoke volumes to me and made me realize that this man was definitely a keeper.

While I was daydreaming about the possibility of spending a lot of time here, Bintu walked back into the room with two champagne glasses filled to the rim with something sparkling.

I smiled. "Where did you get this from? I didn't see you in the kitchen."

He smiled back. "We have a bar around the corner, in the entertainment room."

I took the glass he offered. "Who are you talking about when you say we?"

"I'm talking about me and Fatu."

"Fatu lives here too?" I was somewhat disappointed.

He took a sip from his glass and sat next to me. "Yes, we are roommates."

Hearing this man just tell me that he shared this place with Fatu really turned me off. There was no chance in hell that I would be able to spend a lot of time here. How would I be able to get comfortable? There was nothing better than walking around naked with your man, or fucking him on the kitchen table when you knew that you were there alone, and no one was going to walk in on you. Bintu and Fatu rooming together changed the game for me, and I didn't like it, so I was going to have to do something about it. Either Fatu was going to have to find him somewhere else to go, or Bintu was, especially if we took this thing to another level.

After he and I finished our glasses of champagne, we retired upstairs to his bedroom. Homeboy had the king-sized canopy with tall pillars, and the bed had to be at least three-and-a-half feet high! Cream-colored silk drapes draped from the tops of the pillars to each post on the bed. The cream-and-beige decorative pillows and the matching comforter set were beautiful. It was evident that a woman or an interior decorator incorporated these colors and designs to work together.

After I took inventory of his entire room and made compliments, Bintu took me into his arms and laid me back onto the bed. The comforter was so plush I felt like I was resting on a cloud in heaven.

Bintu removed all of my clothing and kissed every inch of my body while I felt the effects of the alcohol kick in to overdrive. Between the buzz from the champagne and the sparks I felt from Bintu's touch, I knew tonight was going to be a night I'd never forget.

"Come get on top of me," Bintu ordered as he lay naked on his back.

Before I climbed on top of him, I took inventory of his body. His frame was nicely built, but he had a lot of chest hair, and the fact that it was sort of kinky and knotted up kind of turned me off a little. I had always dealt with men who kept that shit cut off because it was not attractive. Somebody needed to tell Bintu that he was not living in the seventies, where cats used to walk around with their shirts unbuttoned to show off their hairy chests. It was not cute.

What was even worse was that Bintu's dick wasn't as big as I thought it would be. It had to be every bit of four-and-a-half to five inches erect. And did I mention that it wasn't circumcised? That was really odd for me. I had never been with a man who had not had the foreskin of his dick carved off. I tried desperately not stare at it, but when Bintu gestured for me to give him some head, I was seriously offended. I was not about to put that thing in my mouth! To be brutally honest, I really didn't want him to stick that thing inside me.

Then a vision of me going on all sorts of trips and shopping sprees with that nigga's money popped into my head. Kira would be hating her ass off if I could pull this nigga off his square and get him to do anything I asked. That would be the ultimate victory for me, since she thought she had it going on when it came to getting cats to take care of her. I had a trick for her ass, though. What I was about to do was some unconventional shit, and it was going to turn this little dick-ass nigga out.

I closed my eyes, put my mouth around Bintu's dick, and went to work. It tasted kind of salty and I gagged a few times, but I held it down like a trooper and successfully got his dick harder than a rock. I estimated his dick was now at the six-inch mark, so it became easier to work with. Seconds later he handed me a condom. I strapped it on him, hopped on board, and rode his dick until he came.

When it was over, Bintu exhaled like he did all the work, but I didn't say a word. I pretended like I came too. Bintu's expression was full of pride like he truly did something, and I was the one suffering from excruciating pain in my knees. It was all good, though. I let him have his moment, because his dick wasn't that bad. Besides, I was gonna be A-OK, especially after all the work I just put in. That nigga was going to treat me like royalty from this day forward, and I couldn't wait.

Gossip Girl

(Kira Speaks)

I got a call from Fatu before I left for work the next morning, thanking me again for coming out to this party. We talked for a bit and then he reminded me about our possible lunch date, so I told him I would call him around noon to confirm. Right after we hung up, I sat back on my bed and thought about how nice of a time I had with him last night. I really felt comfortable being around him, so I could definitely see myself getting to know him on a more personal level.

What I felt uncomfortable about was the fact that when I was ready to call it a night, Nikki refused to leave with me. I guess she felt like that was her opportune time to get to know Bintu. She apparently didn't know—or didn't care—that she was sending him the wrong signal. When you met a man one day and decided to go to his house the next, it gave off the wrong impression. Going home that time of the night with him was a straight-up booty call, but I just hoped she didn't fall prey to it. Since she had not come home at all yet, I knew I would hear about her night when she brought her butt into work.

Later that day Carmen, Rachael, and I were busy with our clients when Miss Mouth Almighty strutted her stuff through the front door of the shop like she was America's Next Top Model. It was a little after eleven o'clock and she had the nerve to come in with a huge smile on her face.

"Hi, ladies," she said and flopped her handbag onto the prepping station.

I ignored her, but that didn't stop Rachael and Carmen from speaking. "What's up with that smile?" Carmen asked.

"Yeah, Nikki, why you smiling so hard?" Rachael asked.

"Because I'm happy, that's why."

Rachael didn't think that was enough information, so she stopped in the middle of styling her client's hair to press Nikki. "Come on now, tell us what happened last night at the party."

"Kira didn't tell you already?" Nikki responded sarcastically.

Annoyed by her cynicism, I asked, "What was I supposed to tell them?"

"Come on, now, Kira. I know you already told them what happened at the party last night."

"Yeah, I told them about what went on with me."

"Oh, so you're telling me that y'all didn't bring my name up?"

"Nikki, you ain't that important!" I snapped. "We have a business to run, so we don't walk around here and talk about you all day long."

"Yeah, whatever!" Nikki sucked her teeth and turned her attention to Rachael. Before she could utter a word, Rachael beat her to the punch.

"Never mind all that. Tell me what happened with you and your friend last night! You know I'm dying to know."

I watched Nikki through my peripheral vision the entire time she and Rachael carried on with their madness. Nikki sat in the styling chair next the prepping station and ran her mouth like there was no tomorrow.

"Girl, you should've seen his apartment," she boasted.

"Was it nice?" Rachael asked.

"Hell yeah! It was some shit you'd see in a magazine."

"Where was it?"

"It's probably downtown," Carmen interjected.

"It is," Nikki confirmed. "And when I tell you that place is on fire, believe me."

"He must've given you a tour of it."

Nikki smiled a naughty smile. "He sure did."

"What else did he give you? Because I know you stayed with him the entire night," Rachael said and smirked.

"You ain't got to go into all that," Carmen blurted out. "Just tell us if he was good or not."

Nikki hesitated for a second and then smiled and said, "He wasn't all that big, but he definitely knows what to do with it."

Rachael's mouth dropped open. "Oh my God! You did it with him for real?"

"Yep, I sure did. I rocked his world too."

Rachael shook her head in disapproval. "I sure hope you didn't give that nigga any head."

"Are you crazy? I just met the man the night before," she said with her mouth twitching, so I knew she was lying. And at that very moment I started to call her ass out and tell her that I knew she was lying. But then I figured, what would be the fucking use? She wanted to play like she was on top of the world, so I just let her live in her fantasy world and remained quiet.

"Did he grab you around the neck or make any subtle movements like he wanted you to do it?" Carmen inquired.

"No."

"Well, did he give some head?" Carmen continued.

Nikki burst into laughter. "No!"

"Well, did you even try to position your body to see if he would do it?" Rachael jumped in.

Nikki laughed harder. "No, I didn't. All we did was kiss each other and make love."

"So, what did y'all do this morning? Did he cook you breakfast?" Rachael continued.

"No, he didn't cook me breakfast, but we drove out to University Boulevard and had brunch in the Village."

"So, do you like him?" Carmen asked.

"Yeah, he's cool."

"Do you see y'all getting serious?" she pressed.

"I'm not sure, but if the timing is right, I'd take a shot at it."

"When are you going to see him again?" Rachael asked.

"He didn't say, but I'm sure it'll be sometime this week."

Nikki continued to run her mouth about her relationship predictions with Bintu. I had a few predictions of my own, especially now that I knew she fucked him on their first date. As far as I was concerned, she could hang it up. He was not going to want to settle down with her. Now she could try and fool herself to believe otherwise, but the truth would be revealed, and it was going to be sooner than she thought. I just hoped that the stunt she pulled last night with Bintu didn't have an effect on how Fatu saw me. I would hate for him to judge me based on the dumb shit Nikki did. But if he did, and tried to play me, then I'd personally rip his fucking head off and tell him where the fuck to go.

After forty minutes of detailed information about how Bintu gave her a wet ass, Nikki finally shut the hell up and started working. Over the next two hours we only said about five words to each other, which was fine with me. Nikki had a chip on her shoulder, and until she got it off, our relationship would remain strained.

I took a break around one PM after I put my last client for the day under the hair dryer. I called Fatu to tell him that I would be available to meet him for a late lunch around three.

"Why so late?" he asked.

"Because I have to wait for my client's hair to dry, so Nikki can braid it, and then I can sew in the weave."

"And that takes two whole hours?"

"Almost."

"OK. Well when you're done, would you meet me at this restaurant called the Aquarium?"

"Where is that?"

"It's downtown on Bagby Street."

"I'm not sure where that is, but don't worry because all I have to do is punch it into my GPS system, and my car will take me straight there."

"Sounds good. I guess I'll see you there."

"Hey, Fatu, wait!" I yelled before he hung up.

"What's the matter?"

"I just wanted to know if I had to wear anything formal."

"Oh, no! It's just a seafood restaurant. Come as you are."

"OK," I said and hung up.

After I finished my last client, I told everyone that I'd see them later. Rachael's nosey ass wanted to know where I was going, so I told her that I was meeting Fatu for lunch at the Aquarium. She and Carmen both started harping on about how nice that place was, and how much I would love it. Nikki didn't say a word and I was glad. Knowing her, she would've said something negative, and I was truly not in the mood for that. Carmen and Rachael wished me well and told me to enjoy myself.

"I will," I assured them, and then left to meet my date.

Big Time Hater

(Nikki Speaks)

Kira always found a way to rub shit in my face, but I refused to let her get to me. She knew she didn't have to broadcast where Fatu was taking her, and I would bet every dime in my pocket that she called him to set up the date after she heard me tell Carmen and Rachael that me and Bintu had brunch together this morning. She was such a fucking hater! Why did she always have to be in the spotlight? Wasn't it enough that Fatu sent his personal shopper to the salon for her to pick out something to wear to his party? I mean, damn! Let me shine sometimes. It was bad enough that I was younger than her, so give me a fucking break already. Her time was up!

During the course of the day I helped Carmen and Rachael prep their clients, and on my downtime, I did some paperwork. By five PM I hadn't heard from Bintu, so I tried to get him on the phone while I was in the back office, but I got his voice mail. I left him a brief message saying that I called to hear his voice, so when he got a moment, I wanted him to call me back. As soon as I hung up my cell phone, it started ringing. My heart pounded because I knew it was Bintu calling me right back.

"Hello," I said without looking at the CallerID.

"What's good, shawty?"

When I heard the country accent, I automatically knew that it wasn't Bintu. This was Neeko, the cat I'd just met yesterday. I forced a smile and said, "I'm good! What's up with you?"

"I'm chilling."

"So what do I owe the pleasure of this phone call?"

"I was calling you to see if you wanted to hang out later."

"Where are you trying to go?"

"I was hoping you'd go out to dinner with me."

"Sure. What time are you talking?"

"What about nine?"

"Nine is cool, but where are you taking me?"

"I don't know, but I'm sure we could ride around and find something."

"OK, that's fine. What are you doing now?"

"Well I'm driving down the beltway so I can make a quick stop at my homeboy's spot."

"Where's your girlfriend?"

"Probably hanging out with her girlfriends."

"So she's letting you hang out tonight?"

"She ain't letting me do a damn thang! I'm doing this because I want to."

Blown away by his arrogance, I said, "OK. You stated your case! How long are you going to be at your homeboy's spot?"

"Not long. Why?"

"No reason. I just asked."

"What are you doing now?"

"I'm down at the salon, sitting in my office, trying to organize a few things."

"Make a lot of money today?"

"What kind of question is that? We've got the best stylists around town, so of course we did," I replied in a cocky manner, dishing out the same amount of egotism he had just dished out to me.

"Who's there with you now?" he asked, obviously not feeding into my haughtiness.

"Both of the stylists we have, but all of us are getting ready to leave."

"And where are you going after you leave there?"

"Home to take a shower so I can see you later."

"Whatcha gon' wear?"

"I'm not sure."

"Do you have any cute little skirts or dresses?"

"Yeah, I have a lot of them."

"Well, wear one of them."

"OK, I will."

Just as I was getting ready to speak again, Neeko cut me off. "Hey, listen, Nikki, I'ma call you back after I holla at my peoples, OK?"

"OK."

After I hung up with Neeko, I was happy to no end. I was going out on a date tonight and I knew I was going to have a good time. He looked like he had money, so I knew he was going to take me somewhere really nice. Now I wasn't gonna fuck him, because I had just fucked Bintu last night and that would be trifling of me to let another man dig up in me the very next night. What I planned to do was eat, talk, and bullshit around until I got tired.

Several minutes later I heard Rachael scream at the top of her lungs. I jumped to my feet and snatched the office door open to see what was going on. I was met by a very tall, masked man pointing a big-ass gun in my face.

"If you scream or make any noise, I'm gon' kill you right on the spot," he warned me.

"What's going on?" I managed to utter, my voice quivering.

"Shut the fuck up! I'm the one that's gonna ask the questions."

I tried desperately to swallow the knot caught in the center of my throat. Instead of breaking down, I stood there and waited for him to tell me why he was there.

"Get back in the office and stand up against the wall," he instructed. I did as he told me. Moments later, Carmen and Rachael appeared around the corner with tears rolling down their faces. I wanted so badly to say something to them, but I knew I would be putting my life in jeopardy, so I only gave them eye contact.

"Get over there by the wall and stand next to her," another masked man told Carmen and Rachael.

I couldn't tell you who these two men were, and I wouldn't be able to make out their voices if I ever heard them again, because it seemed like everybody in Houston sounded just alike. The only difference between the two of them was that the guy who stuck the gun in my face was taller than the one who had Carmen and Rachael at gunpoint. I just wanted to give them what they wanted and let them leave without any problems. I just hoped Carmen and Rachael felt the same way.

"Where's the money?" the taller guy asked. His voice was intimidating and sadistic, and I knew he meant business.

I spoke up first. "What money are you talking about?"

"I'm talking about all the money y'all made today. I want y'all to empty your pockets and put everything on the table."

All three of us dug deep into our pockets and our handbags and pulled out every dollar we had, and laid the money on my desk. I couldn't be too sure, but I knew Carmen and Rachael had to put down every bit of two grand a piece, considering they both had a couple of sew-ins to do, along with three lace-front wigs. Thank God I only added about

$123 to the stack because if I would've had one penny more, I probably would have freaked out by now.

"Take off your jewelry too," he demanded.

I almost shit on myself. I had a seven-thousand-dollar diamond necklace around my neck, twenty-six-hundred-dollar diamond stud earrings in my ears, and a four-thousand-dollar Rolex on my wrist. I'd just copped these three pieces with the dough I took from Quincy's crib right before I left Virginia, and I wasn't trying to part with them. However, I knew that if I didn't, they'd take my jewelry and try to make me pay for trying to keep it. I wasn't willing to go through all of that so I carefully took off my jewelry and laid the pieces across the desk, beside the money.

Rachael had on a one-and-a-half-carat diamond wedding set that looked like it probably cost about two-thousand-dollars, and a pair of gold hoop earrings. She removed everything and set it beside my things. Carmen had on a ton of some expensive shit. She had on a five-carat diamond engagement ring, a platinum-and-diamond bracelet, a pair of white gold-and-diamond hoop earrings, and a platinum chain flooded with black diamonds that happened to belong to her fiancé, Xavier. Carmen had told us that chain cost forty-thousand-dollars. From what I'd heard, Xavier was a big-time dealer out here in these streets, and he was known not to be fucked with, so I knew he was going to be furious when he found out that these motherfuckers took his shit. Carmen knew this too, so before she made a move to take off any of her jewelry, she got up the nerve to give these cats a choice.

"Before I take off all my jewelry, I just wanted to let you know that my fiancé's name is X, and if he finds out that I was robbed and his chain was taken, he ain't gonna be happy."

The leader stepped in Carmen's face and stood toe to toe with her. "Do you think I give a fuck about that nigga you fuck with?"

Her voice was barely audible. "Well, please don't take my ring! We're about to get married in a couple of months."

"I don't give a damn! Now take that shit off before I go upside your motherfucking head with this pistol," he threatened.

Carmen knew that the nigga was serious, so she didn't want to take any more chances with him. Carmen took off all her things and set them on top of the desk, but that wasn't good enough for the nigga who was doing all of the demanding. He wanted her to stuff everything on the desk into a black bag he retrieved from his back pants pocket. After that was done, he picked up the loaded bag, looked at his partner, and said, "Take those two into the bathroom and lock them up in there while I have a few moments with this one." He gestured at Carmen.

"Whatcha about to do?" the other guy asked.

"I got to take care of some business with big mouth right here."

I got an uneasy feeling. I knew that the "business" couldn't mean nothing else but rape, so I got up the nerve to speak up. "Is that n-necessary?" I stuttered. "I mean, the owner of this place has been out all day, so he should be on his way back to lock up the place, and I would hate for this to get any uglier."

"Yeah, man, she's right," the second guy agreed. "We got what we came here for, so let's get the hell out of here!"

The leader hesitated. "Yeah, a'ight," he finally said. I let out a silent sigh of relief. Then the leader fondled Carmen's breasts. "Damn, shawty, these joints are soft as hell!" he laughed. "Count your blessings, because if me and my homeboy here wasn't in a rush, I would've had some fun with you."

Carmen stood frozen with a humiliated expression on her face. I knew she was mortified and wanted so badly to spit in his face, but the fear of losing her life behind it probably crossed her mind, because she looked the other way. All Rachael and I did was stand there in shock.

"Come on, man, let's go!" the second guy insisted as he walked backward out of the office.

"Slow your ass down, man!" the leader snapped. "We got to lock their asses up in the bathroom before we go anywhere."

The other guy peeped out into the hallway. "Ain't no lock on the outside of the bathroom door, so we gon' have to leave 'em in here."

"A'ight. Well, come on." The leader yanked the phone cable out of the wall so that there was no way that we would have been able to plug it back up to use it. He made us give him our cellular phones and demanded that I hand over the keys to the shop. "They're in the top left drawer of the desk," I told him.

They backed out of the office, closed the door, and locked us inside. The feeling we all had once those bastards left our presence was indescribable. Rachael looked like she was about to pass out, and Carmen acted like she was about to have a meltdown. Her eyes welled up with tears and before I could utter one word, she began to sob uncontrollably. I immediately embraced her.

"Go ahead and let it out," I encouraged her as I held her tightly. Carmen was as stiff as a board. I knew she was suffering from emotional defeat because I could not get her to embrace me for nothing in the world. The fact that we were locked up in that small-ass room didn't help the situation at all. Rachael made it even worse by complaining about how claustrophobic she was and that if somebody didn't come to let us out soon, then she was going to have a panic attack.

"Can you please calm the hell down?" I roared. "Remember, you aren't the only one stuck in here."

"How can I be calm when I have a medical condition?"

"I'm not a fucking doctor! So you're going to have to come up with a solution on your own," I snapped.

Rachael wasn't trying to hear me. She wanted out of that office more than we could imagine, so she started banging on the wall, hoping it would get the women's attention from the African braiding shop next door. Unfortunately for us, their music was blasting so loudly that there was no way they were going to hear us.

We sat there and prayed that someone would come by and let us out. We knew Carmen's fiancé wouldn't be stopping by because she had not spoken to him all day. Normally when he did that, she said, he was out taking care of business, so the only other people that would have a remote interest in stopping by would be Kira or Peter, Rachael's husband. We hoped that one of them came soon, because I didn't think we'd last long in there.

New Love

(Kira Speaks)

The Aquarium restaurant was so nice and cozy! Fatu and I were seated around an elaborate aquarium filled with over one hundred species of colorful fish and marine life. It was truly unbelievable. What really stood out for me was the array of seafood entrees. Fatu had the sixteen-spice tuna with pan-fried green beans, and I had a filet mignon with Thai pepper shrimp and a vegetable medley. To wash everything down, we sipped on a bottle of white Zinfandel and talked ourselves to death. Once again, I could say that I truly enjoyed myself in his company.

After our lunch date ended, he whipped out his titanium American Express card to pay for our food and then he invited me to come back to his nightclub with him to share a bottle of champagne. I declined his offer because I wasn't dressed appropriately, but when he assured me that I would be hanging out with him in his back office, I conceded.

The ambiance at the club was pleasant. It was around five o'clock, so there weren't any partygoers there as of yet. A couple of his employees ran around rearranging and setting up things before the crowd started pouring in. On our way to his office, Fatu made a few small requests to several other employees, but there was one particular chick he felt the need to put on blast. I heard him call her Shelby. Shelby was an average-looking, brown-skinned woman with dreadlocks pulled back into a ponytail. She was voluptuous in size, but she wore it well. Her attitude needed a makeover, though, and Fatu felt the need to give it to her. I stood by the bar and watched those two go at it.

"Why do I have to always play these games with you?" Fatu asked her. "Just do your job, and I'll start taking you a little more seriously."

"If you would live up to your word, then we wouldn't be having this conversation!" Shelby roared back.

"Do you like working here?" he snapped.

"What kind of question is that? You know I love my job. I just can't stand working for the pennies you give me. Now, if you go ahead and give me that raise you promised me some time ago, we'd all be able to get along again."

Fatu stood there for a second as if he was running a few numbers through his mind, and then suddenly said, "I'm sorry, but I can't accommodate that request right now. Business has been really slow this quarter. However, if things pick up between now and next quarter, then I'll gladly give you that raise."

Not at all happy by Fatu's response, Shelby lashed out at him and said, "Fatu, that's bullshit and you know it! Business is fine! But let's just say that it wasn't." Her voice got more agitated. "A two-dollar-an-hour raise wouldn't hurt you, especially with all that illegal shit y'all are doing in here! I'm not stupid! I know y'all selling more than alcohol around here."

"All right, Shelby, that's enough," Fatu warned her. "If I hear another word from you, then I'm going to have you escorted out of here."

"Fatu, do you think I really care? Escort me out of here, because I quit!" She stormed away to the bar where she went to retrieve her handbag. Right before she opened the front door to leave, she turned around and said, "You better watch your back, you cheap-ass immigrant!"

Fatu stood there in disbelief after Shelby bailed on him. I sat there on the bar stool in complete silence. I knew he probably felt awkward since I witnessed one of his employees embarrass the hell out of him, so I tried to force myself to say something to break the tension barrier, but I couldn't get my mouth to open for nothing. Several seconds later, Fatu came around to me. "Come on. Let's go back into my office." He helped me down from the bar stool. "I'm sorry about all of that. I really wish you would not have witnessed that."

"It's OK," I assured him as he escorted me in the direction of his office. But on some real shit, I began to wonder if the shit Shelby said was true. I mean, why else would she make that accusation? I was sure she had been working here for some time, so I knew she must have seen a lot of underhanded shit. But whether it was drugs or stolen merchandise, I didn't want any part in it. And to make sure I didn't get involved, I was gonna keep my eyes and ears open, because this nigga right here wasn't worth me going to prison behind.

Once inside his office, I took a seat on Fatu's lounge chair while he sat behind his desk. "Give me one second while I check my messages," he said.

"Take your time," I replied and sat back. My eyes wandered around the room and landed on his security monitors. He had five huge closed-circuit monitors, and all of them were mounted on the wall directly in front of his desk. The screens had to be every bit of forty-two inches, because you could see every move a person made without squinting your eyes. Fatu had the bar area and kitchen monitored, and he had cameras over the exits, including the alleyway in the back of the club where he received his shipments, and inside his wine cellar.

I couldn't see any movement in the shipment area of the cellar, but there was plenty of movement in the other parts of the club. One area in particular had a whole lot going on. Bintu was groping some big-booty chick in the kitchen, near the sink. She was giggling her silly ass off while he kissed her neck and his hands got lost inside her panties. There was no sound to the video, but it didn't matter because their actions told it all. Before I could even blink, Bintu flipped homegirl around so that her ass was facing him, unzipped his pants, lifted her skirt, and then he went in for the kill.

I couldn't fucking believe it. This nigga actually went inside this chick without a fucking condom! To know that Nikki just fucked him made me sick to my damn stomach. I wondered if she had enough sense to make him strap up. If she didn't, I really felt sorry for her, because whether she knew it, Bintu was dangerous and reckless. Not only that, the nigga didn't have any regard for anyone but himself. I just hoped that Nikki didn't think she was going to be walking down the aisle with that cat, because from the looks of it, Bintu preferred the stick-and-move lifestyle better.

Fatu made a comment to me, but since I was so preoccupied with the activity on the monitor, I didn't hear him. Fatu snatched open the top drawer to his desk, fumbled with the remote control to the monitor, and powered down that particular monitor after several tries. Sweat beaded his forehead and he probably apologized to me over twenty times, but after I told him for the twentieth time that there was no need to apologize, he got the picture. A few minutes later Fatu excused himself.

"Take your time," I said as I watched him walk out of his office. I already knew where he was going. I could tell he was pissed off by Bintu's actions, and I knew he was going to straighten out his brother. I had the urge to turn the monitor back on so I could watch how Fatu was going to handle this situation, but then I got worried about getting caught, so I elected not to do it.

While I waited patiently for Fatu's return, I couldn't help but wonder what illegal stuff he was into. The very first thing that popped into my head was drugs. But from the looks of things, he didn't strike me as a drug dealer. I'd been dealing with hustlers all my life, it seemed, so I knew what type of niggas they were. Fatu may have been dealing with stolen goods of some kind. Maybe he was dealing in expensive stolen cars or something. Whatever it was, it had to be bringing him in a lot of dough, because any nigga that would shell out eleven thousand dollars for two outfits and two pairs of shoes the day after he met a chick had to be making some power moves.

"I'm back!" Fatu smiled as he peeped his head around the door.

Even though I was still feeling somewhat awkward, I smiled anyway. "Did you handle your business?" I asked.

He hesitated a bit, like I had just hit him below the belt. "Yeah, I handled it. And like I said before, I am truly sorry."

"It's OK."

"So, would you like to have another drink?"

"No, I'm afraid I'm not in the mood for one now."

"Well, is there anything I can get you?" he pressed.

"No, I'm fine," I assured him and stood to leave. I felt like I had been there long enough and overstayed my welcome, so it was time to go.

"I thought you and I were going to share a bottle of champagne?"

"I know, I know. But I'm a little burnt out, so I'm gonna run on home."

"Is there anything I can do to change your mind?"

I walked toward the office door. "Not tonight."

"Well, can I walk you to your car?"

"Sure."

Fatu raced to open the door for me.

We had to walk back through the bar area of the club to get to the front door. When we got within four feet of it, Bintu strolled his nasty ass out of the coat room, which was right by the front entrance, and he was holding a female's jacket in his hand. He gave me this stupid look like he didn't know what to say to me. I looked him directly in his face and made him acknowledge me.

"How you doing?" I asked.

With the cheesiest expression he could find, he replied, "I'm doing fine, Kira. How are you?"

"I'm OK. Have you spoken with Nikki since y'all had brunch this morning?"

"No, I haven't, but I intend to call her after I wrap up things around here." He clutched the woman's jacket tightly.

I glanced at the jacket and then back at him. I really didn't have anything else to say to this nigga, but I felt like it was necessary to give him the impression that I was going to tell Nikki about his little rendezvous with that trifling-ass chicken head. "Well, I'll be sure to tell her that I saw you."

"OK," he said and walked off.

I shook my head with disgust and headed out the door. Fatu followed me like a dog in heat. "You're not gonna tell your cousin about what happened, are you?" he asked.

I stopped in my tracks and looked at him like he was crazy. "Am I not supposed to?"

"Listen, Kira, I can't tell you what to do, but I don't think it would be a good idea to tell Nikki about the situation with Bintu and that other woman."

"I understand what you're saying, but Nikki is my family. I am all she has, so I will not sit back and allow her to get caught up in some bullshit with your brother. I mean, if your brother wants to go and fuck around with different chicks, then that's his business. But when my cousin is caught in the middle of that mess, then I have to say something."

Fatu gently grabbed my hands. "Kira, please don't get involved with their relationship."

"I didn't know they had one," I snapped.

"You know what I'm talking about," he said calmly. "I like you a lot, and I want to get to know you better. But if you start interfering in their business, then that's going to lead to a major disaster."

I stood by my car and listened to Fatu's point of view. It made a lot of sense, but at the end of the day my loyalty to Nikki outweighed everything he said, so she and I would definitely have a long talk when I got home. I just hoped she didn't take this thing to heart, because niggas like Bintu came a dime a dozen, so there were plenty left out there.

Before I got in my car, I lied to Fatu and told him that I wouldn't mention one word about what I saw earlier. I only did this because he acted like he wasn't going to let me leave if I didn't side with him. Little did he know that I couldn't hold water when it came to matters of the heart. That was just how I was, so he could take it or leave it.

When I arrived home I noticed that Nikki's car wasn't there. As soon as I wound down a bit, I called her cellular phone to see where she was. When she didn't answer, I immediately called the salon. The phone to the shop rang about five times before the answering machine picked up, so I automatically assumed that she either just left, or she didn't want to be bothered. Whatever it was, it really didn't matter because I knew I was going to have a chance to talk to her. Eventually I sat back on my living room sofa and thought about exactly what I was going to tell her. I also knew that I had to have her promise that she'd keep everything that I told her to herself.

Whether or not she realized it, she could take this thing and use it to her advantage. Niggas acted so stupid when they got caught doing something they weren't supposed to be doing! That was why it was important for the woman not to get upset and act like a fool. We had to take that very thing the men did to hurt us and turn the tables around to manipulate them. My late husband Ricky taught me that lesson.

I remembered back when he used to cheat on me with some of the nastiest chicks he could find. He had a couple babies by them too. But I didn't let that bullshit get me all bent out of shape. I could have divorced him on so many occasions, but I played it smart and stuck him where it hurt—his pockets—and kept it moving. Believe me, that nigga couldn't see the forest for the trees because of all the shit he was in. That was why I was able to walk away with over three hundred thousand dollars from his stash. Thanks to Russ, I didn't keep it long, but, hey, what could I say? You lived and you learned. I just hoped Nikki could do the same.

Four Hours Later

(Nikki Speaks)

All three of us sat in the back office for what seemed like forever. The whole time we were caged up, Carmen and I had to endure Rachael's fucking phobia issues. Thank God for her husband, though. Peter knew that she was supposed to be at home by seven so they could go to their eight o'clock dinner reservation, so when she didn't show up or answer her phone after an hour and a half of him trying to reach her, he brought his butt down to the shop to see what was going on. He later told us that when he pulled up to the parking lot and saw Rachael's car parked outside, his first thought was to curse her ass out. But then he noticed how dark it was inside the shop and immediately forgot all about ripping her apart and started worrying. Why would all of our cars be parked outside while the lights were out? It just didn't make sense to him. What was even scarier for him was when he tried the front door and it was unlocked. He thought that when he walked inside he was going to find all of us dead. When he heard our voices, he told us he let out a sigh of relief.

"Rachael, baby, is that you back there?" we heard Peter ask.

Rachael immediately recognized her husband's voice and damn near broke down the office door to get through it. "Yes, baby, it's me!

We're locked up back in the office," she yelled.

"Yeah, Peter, you're going to have to find a screwdriver or something to take off lock," I interjected.

Carmen came back to life that instant. "Tell him I have one in the top drawer of my station, buried underneath a bunch of pink curling rods."

"Peter, go to Carmen's station and get that screwdriver out of her top drawer. There's a bunch of pink curling rods piled on top of it," I instructed through the door.

Before he went to get the screwdriver from Carmen's station, he wanted to know how we got locked up in the office in the first place. Rachael started running off at the mouth, so Carmen looked at her and said, "Can you let him get us out of here before you go into all that?"

Rachael was downright appalled by Carmen's sudden outburst. Her expression told it all. Peter heard Carmen scream on Rachael, but instead of getting in the middle of the commotion, he went and got the screwdriver. It took him about five minutes to unscrew the lock from the door, and the moment the door opened, I felt a sense of relief. I sprinted out of the office first. Carmen and Rachael followed suit. Rachael ran straight into her husband's arms and started reiterating the whole robbery episode. Peter was floored by what she was telling him. As badly as I wanted to get in on their conversation, I thought it would do me more justice to call the police so we could all make a report.

While we sat and waited for the police to show up, I called the house and got Kira on the line. "Girl, you aren't going to believe what happened after you left the shop," I said.

"What happened?"

"A couple of niggas wearing ski masks ran up in the shop and robbed us."

"Who is us?" Kira asked frantically.

"I'm talking about me, Carmen, and Rachael."

"Oh, my God! What did they take?"

Disgusted by the reality of it all, I sighed and said, "They took all our money, our jewelry, and our fucking cell phones."

"They took y'all's money and jewelry?" Kira snapped. She was furious.

"Yes! And right after they took our shit from us, they locked us up in the back office and took my keys."

"What the fuck!" Kira screamed through the receiver. "They took your keys too?"

"Yeah."

Kira became livid. "So you're telling me that those bastards have a key to the shop?"

"Yeah, and they got the keys to my fucking car too!" I roared.

"Did you call the police?"

"Yes, I did."

"All right. Well I'll be up there in a minute."

"Can you please bring me my spare car key from the key holder in the kitchen?" I asked.

Instead of responding to my question, that bitch had the audacity to hang up the phone in my ear without giving me any warning. I knew she was upset about those niggas having the keys to her shop, but what about my car? Unlike her, I paid cash for my whip and I must say that it cost more than anything in this damn place, so she needed to calm the hell down and stop thinking about herself. It wasn't becoming at all.

Right after I hung up the phone, I walked outside to see if those niggas drove off with my car, but when I saw it parked in the same spot, I was truly relieved. I went right back into the shop and took a seat at my station. I noticed Rachael was still running her mouth to Peter while Carmen was on the shop phone near her station. She was an emotional wreck. I heard her crying through the phone to Xavier about the whole thing, including the robbery and how one of the guys was about to rape her until the other one stopped him.

I couldn't tell you what X said to Carmen, but I could tell you that he was screaming his poor heart out. Homeboy was pissed, so I knew some shit was about pop off. Judging from the things Carmen had mentioned about him in the past, I believed that X was going to find out who robbed us, especially since his forty-thousand-dollar platinum-and-black diamond chain was taken in the process. I just hoped he found them before they had a chance to pawn my shit.

Before they hung up with each other, I overheard Carmen telling X that he needed to get up there right now. From the urgency in her voice, there was no doubt in my mind that X was going to come bursting through the shop door at any given moment.

Shit Got Even Worse

(Kira Speaks)

I almost had an anxiety attack on my way to the shop. All I could think about was what kind of shape my salon was in, not to mention the fact that those niggas had keys to unlock the doors of my establishment. Call me cruel, but I couldn't worry about the fact that Carmen, Nikki, and Rachael got robbed. Shit, that little bit of crap they had could be replaced. But the fact that my salon had been invaded by those Viking-ass niggas could not be taken back. I knew I should have been a little more sensitive about what happened to them, but those hoes were fine. Those niggas left them in one piece, so I couldn't worry about them. I needed to focus on my damn salon.

Upon my arrival, I was thrown over the edge when I walked into the salon and was greeted by Carmen's fiancé Xavier and a couple of police officers—one male, one female. X was cursing his ass off and throwing a lot of threats around, saying he was going to take care of the niggas who robbed Carmen. As quickly as he said it, the police shut down his silly ass. "Sir, we know that you're upset about all this, but if you take matters into your own hands, you'd only complicate the situation," the male officer told him.

"I ain't gon' complicate a damn thing. All I'ma do is rectify it because those niggas took something that belonged to me, and I can't have them flossin' it around town like it's theirs. I worked too hard for that shit! So them niggas are gonna either give it back, or they're gonna have to pay for it," he protested. I saw right through him. He had two of his flunkies in the shop with him, so I knew he was putting on a show for them.

"Did you have your diamond necklace insured?" the same officer asked.

"What street nigga you know does that?" X snapped. "Shiit, I don't even have health insurance."

"Well, it sounds like you need to make a call to your local insurance agent," I interjected.

"And you are?" the male officer asked.

I ignored him and approached the female officer. "My name is Kira Walters, the other owner of this salon. I want to thank you for coming by."

"That's what we're here for," she assured me.

Xavier sucked his teeth. "Man, ain't nobody trying to hear all that. Get my damn chain back, and then you'd be doing your job."

The female officer ignored him, but the male officer chimed in. "Sir, we all know you're upset, but you're gonna have to calm down so we can conduct this investigation properly."

Hearing the intensity in the officer's voice, Xavier stepped down from his high horse and took a backseat. Carmen grabbed his arm and pulled him back toward her. Both of the police officers took everyone's statements, left us their business cards, and assured us that they would do their best to find the robbers and bring them to justice. I thanked them both and saw them to the door.

After they left, Xavier grabbed Carmen's handbag from her lap and said, "Get the rest of your shit so we can get the hell out of here!"

Carmen started gathering all her curling irons, combs, brushes, rollers, and hair products and began placing them into a box. I was shocked by her actions.

"What's going on? Are you leaving for good?" I asked.

"Yep, she sure is. But you would have known that if you would have been here just a little bit sooner," Nikki interjected sarcastically.

"Please shut the hell up, Nikki, and stay in your damn place! No one was talking to you!"

"I ain't got to do a damn thing! I'm so sick of your snooty ass, always walking around here like your shit doesn't stink while we're 'round here getting the fucked-up end of the stick." She chuckled. "Shit, I don't blame Carmen for leaving. Niggas running up in here like their fucking minds are bad, manhandling us and shit and we ain't got nothing in here to protect us."

"Well, why aren't you packing your shit too?" I roared.

"I will, as soon as I find me a shop," she fired back.

"Why does it have to be a shop? I mean, it's not like you can do hair anyway. So why would you even waste your time?" I said and paused, and then I snapped my fingers like a thought suddenly came to mind. "Oh, yeah, I forgot, you are always to trying to do the same shit I do. I wear all designer name clothes, now you're trying to cop the same shit. I got a new whip, you got the exact same one."

"Yep, but I paid cash for mine. Too bad you couldn't do the same," Nikki snapped back.

"It doesn't matter, Nikki, because you're still a fucking hater!"

"Nah, bitch! You're the fucking hater! And for your information, I can do hair. And as soon as I get my license and open up a shop, I'm gon' show your dumb ass how to really run a salon."

"Yeah, what the fuck ever! I wish you would hurry up," I replied and turned toward Carmen because I really had had enough of Nikki's mouth. Carmen held her head down the entire time she was arranging the items in the box. It didn't matter to me, though, because I knew she was going to hear every word I had to say. "Is there anything I can do or say that would make you stay?" I asked.

"I'm sorry, Kira, but that ain't gon' happen," Xavier yelled from the front door. "She's going to open up her own salon in the part of town where I be at, so I ain't got to worry about this shit ever happening again."

"Is this what you want?" I whispered to her.

Carmen looked at me with tears falling from her eyes. "One of the guys was getting ready to rape me until the other one talked him out of it," she whispered back.

Hearing her say those words hit me like a ton of bricks, so I immediately embraced her. "Oh my God! I didn't know. I am so sorry."

"Don't worry about it. It's not your fault."

I continued to hold her because I felt her pain. I guess Xavier wasn't feeling my gesture because he walked over to us and broke us apart. "Come on, now, enough of that shit! We gotta go." He tugged on Carmen's arm. "Grab her stuff," he instructed one of his boys.

I let her go and watched her as X escorted her out of the shop. "Call me," I shouted.

Carmen looked back at me. "I will."

While I watched the last guy close the door behind them, Rachael told her husband to go out to the car and wait for her. She looked at me and said, "Do you have a clause on your insurance policy that would allow me to file a claim for theft?"

I looked at her like she was out of her damn mind. "No, I don't."

"So you mean to tell me that my husband is going to have to come out of his own pocket to replace my wedding band set?"

"I'm afraid so. The policy I have for my business will only cover damages lost in fire or a natural disaster."

Rachael sighed heavily and stormed off. "Well, somebody is going to have to pay for my loss, because my husband shouldn't have to."

"Wait a minute! You mean to tell me that your husband didn't purchase any insurance on your ring when he bought it?"

"No, I didn't," Peter blurted out.

"Well, I'm sorry to hear that, but that was truly a bad judgment call."

"You're right, Kira, it may have been a bad call on our part," Rachael acknowledged. "But who thinks that one day while she's working, two big-ass guys are going to barge in and rob her? You would think that your workplace is a safe haven, like your home."

"I agree," I said, "but that robbery that happened today can happen anywhere."

"Yeah, you're right, but the only difference is that I looked at this place as my second home, and now I can't say that I feel that way anymore."

"Well, I am sorry that you feel that way, Rachael." I watched as she walked toward her husband. All she did was shake her head in dismay and leave.

Right after she left, I went into my back office and made a call to an after-hours locksmith. When I returned to the service area, I noticed that Nikki had left. Thank God, because I couldn't take being around her much longer, and if she would've said another word to me, we would have been knocking down everything in here.

I made sure the locksmith wasn't located too far away, because I didn't like the feeling of being there all by myself while someone else had the keys. After the locksmith arrives and was switching my locks, I tried to call Fatu, but one of his bartenders told me that he was in the middle of a meeting. I left a message to have him call me when he was free.

It only took the locksmith twenty minutes to change my locks. I paid him, set my alarm, and had him walk me to my car. Before I drove off, I looked back at the shop and wondered to myself, *Who in the hell could've robbed me?*

I couldn't help but glance over at Sophie's shop. All the lights were out, but they weren't out when I'd first arrived, so it wouldn't shock me if they had something to do with it, or saw the perpetrators who did it. God only knew. Hopefully we would soon find out for ourselves.

Something Just Ain't Right
(Nikki Speaks)

I didn't know what the fuck was going on with Bintu. He hadn't returned any of my calls. The last time I'd spoken to him was the morning after we left his apartment and had brunch, which was two days ago, and I was pissed. I sat at my station twiddling my thumbs while Kira's stupid ass styled her client's hair and Rachael washed a perm out of one of her client's heads. Everybody was acting like they were so fucking busy, but I saw right through that shit. I mean, I looked at Rachael's silly ass. She was mad as hell that Kira wouldn't reimburse her for her loss, which I thought was ridiculous of her to ask, but it seemed like she was trying to cope with it. Sadly for her, though, she had nowhere else to go right then, so she was stuck like Chuck and couldn't do a damn thing about it.

Carmen, however, wasn't playing. Her man told Kira that she wasn't coming back, and he meant that shit too. Even though Carmen didn't have a shop to call her own at that point, I was sure that she and X were working on that. I definitely wished her the best, because she was cool, and I would love to work with her again.

Several hours passed and I was still unable to get in touch with Bintu, so I took a ride over to the nightclub. I didn't see his car, so I immediately busted a U-turn and headed over to his apartment. I knew he had to be there, so that was where I went, because I needed some answers.

Upon my arrival I did the curbside valet parking and then tried to board the elevator, but the tall, blonde, female concierge stopped me in my tracks. "Excuse me," the woman said, "are you a new resident I'm not aware of?"

Embarrassed by the way she approached me, I smiled to kind of play it off and then I said, "No, I'm not a resident. But my boyfriend is."

"And who might that be?"

"His name is Bintu."

"Does this Bintu have a last name?"

"Yes, it's Oduka. His apartment is on the—"

"I know what floor he lives on," she interjected, "but since you're not a resident, you can't just go up to his apartment without being announced."

"I just wanted to see if he was home because I've been trying to contact him all day."

"Oh, so he's not expecting you?"

"No, he's not."

"Well, come with me to the front desk and I'll see if I can get him on the phone." She gestured for me to walk ahead of her. I was frustrated and hesitated a bit, because I didn't want her to give Bintu the heads up that I was downstairs. I honestly wanted the chance to walk up on him and find out why he'd been avoiding me, but I saw that that wasn't going to happen. I sighed once more and went over to the front desk. The concierge dialed the extension to Bintu's apartment. I waited patiently while she prepared to announce that I was in the building. To my surprise, when someone answered on the other end, she immediately turned her back to me and started whispering. I couldn't hear a damn word she was saying and was getting more pissed by the second.

"Well, is he there?" I blurted out.

She ignored my question and hung up the phone. With a cheesy-ass expression, she said, "I was just told that he wasn't in."

"Who were you just talking to?" I growled.

"I'm not at liberty to say."

"What is the big fucking secret? It couldn't have been nobody but Bintu or his brother Fatu, unless there's somebody else up there that I don't know about!"

"Ma'am, I'm afraid you're going to have to leave."

"I'm not going anywhere until you tell me who you were just talking to," I protested.

"And I told you, I'm not at liberty to say."

"That's bullshit and you know it," I snapped. "Trying to play fucking mind games with me. I'm not stupid! I know you were talking to Bintu because you would not have turned your back to me and started whispering."

"Ma'am, I'm only going to tell you to leave one more time."

"And what's going to happen if I don't?"

"I'm going to call security, and if you like, I could get you banned from this building indefinitely."

I stared at her in shock. "You can't do that!"

"Yes, I can. Now the best thing you can do right now is take a walk before this thing gets out of hand."

"Yeah, what the fuck ever!" I stormed off because I really didn't want to get thrown out of there. She probably could have banned me from coming back, and I didn't want that to happen. I got my car from the valet attendant and got the hell out of there before I did something I'd probably regret later.

During my drive back to the shop, all I could think about was what the hell was going on with Bintu? I mean, was he trying to play me or what? I just couldn't believe that the first night we spent together was a one-night stand, especially after all the talk we had about spending more time together so we could get to know each other more. Whatever was going on with him was totally a mystery to me, but I was determined to find out what it was.

Dropping a Bombshell
(Kira Speaks)

Nikki had probably been gone from the shop for about an hour or so, and it was so peaceful while she was away. When she came stomping back through that front door, it seemed like all the peace we had just evaporated into thin air. She had a chip on her shoulder before she left, and now it seemed like her whole world had just fallen apart. She threw shit around like her mind was going bad, so I had to say something to her.

"Nikki, could you please stop throwing your things around? It's irritating everyone in the shop."

"You mean it's irritating you," she struck back.

I sighed because I saw where this conversation was going. "Yeah, all right. It's whatever you say." I went back to rolling up my client's hair, but Nikki didn't want to let it go.

"You think it's all about you, huh?" she asked.

"What are you talking about now?"

"You know what I'm talking about." She took a couple steps toward me.

"Nikki, you need to chill out," I warned her.

She immediately got cocky. "What if I don't?"

"Come on, now, Nikki! What is it with you and all your drama? It was so quiet while you were gone. And now you're back and have started up some shit, and you've only been here for about sixty seconds."

"And so what?" she snapped. "Has it ever crossed your mind that I'm tired of a lot of bullshit that goes on around here?"

"You're the one who's causing it," I retorted.

"Well, since I'm the one causing it, then tell me who's been running their fucking mouth?"

"Running their mouth off to who?" I asked in confusion.

"To Bintu."

"I don't understand what you're asking me. I mean, what does Bintu have to do with all the drama you create around here?"

"Kira, don't be a fucking bitch! You know what I'm talking about! You know you been running your mouth to Bintu about me, and that's why he won't return any of my phone calls."

I looked at her in confusion. "That's bull! I haven't said shit to Bintu. As a matter-of-fact, I only saw him once, and that was at the club after me and Fatu had lunch. When I saw him then, we didn't have much to say to each other."

"Do you think I believe that shit you're telling me? You're a hater and you've been hating on me since the beginning, telling me not to get involved with him because of how possessive African men are, and that they're very controlling. And now look at you, damn near broke your neck to hop in bed with Fatu."

"That's a motherfucking lie! I didn't break my neck to do shit! That nigga spent close to twenty grand on me before I even kissed him. Can't say the same about your ten-dollar, drink-getting ass! 'Round here trying to front on me like I'm hating on you! Last time I checked, you didn't have shit for me to hate on! You live with me and I have way more expensive shit in my closet than you do. Remember, Nikki, I am the one who introduced you to this lifestyle. You didn't know shit about fucking with cats with a whole ass full of money. So show some respect, please, because you'll never be able to get to my level. You're too naïve and stupid! And on a more serious note, I could care less about your relationship with Bintu. I've got my own shit to deal with."

"Oh, bitch, you can sell someone else that bullshit! I know what time it is with your ass! You've always been jealous of me since we were kids. You think I don't remember you telling me how you wished you had supportive parents like mine and you wished that you lived in the house that we had and that you wished you could've went to college too? Yeah, you thought I forgot! But I didn't. So sell somebody else that shit about me wanting to be like you, because as far as I can remember, it's been the other way around."

I chuckled. "Nikki, no you didn't go way back there."

"Yep, I sure did, because you think you're hot shit and that everybody wants to be like you. But let me be the first to say that that is not the case. You are not all that! And if Brian was still alive today he'd sure vouch for me and tell you that my pussy was better than yours."

Shocked by her words, my veins damn near popped out of my head. I could not believe this bitch just came out her mouth and said that motherfucking shit in front of everybody. I mean, now how could I come back on that?

"Don't stand there looking stupid! Face it, your pussy is whack! Brian knew it and so did your late husband Ricky, and that's why he fucked every chick in your last shop!"

Hearing Nikki's words tumble out of her mouth made my blood boil, and I was two seconds from punching her in her fucking mouth. "Look, Nikki, I've heard enough. Let's just drop this conversation right now!" I demanded.

"What, ya ashamed?" She laughed. "Yeah, bitch! The joke's on your silly ass now!"

Instead of responding to Nikki's loud outburst, I just stood there in silence. All I could think about was how humiliated she was making me feel in front of everyone. I was screaming inside and hate was building up in me at a rapid pace. The first thing that came to mind was to grab her around her fucking throat and choke the hell out of her. But then I figured that wouldn't be smart on my part. I had clients watching me, so I had to remain professional at whatever cost.

"Nikki, I said let's drop it," I said in a calm tone, trying to let on that she had won the argument.

"I ain't gon' drop it until you tell me what's up! I know you know something."

I burst into laughter to keep from smacking the hell out of her. "Girl, you are really tripping right now."

Nikki took two more steps toward me. "I don't think this shit is funny!"

"Nikki, you better go back over to your station and have a seat before it gets really ugly up in here. I am not feeling too safe with you walking up on me like that, especially while I'm servicing a customer."

"Do you think I care about your fucking customer?" She took yet another step toward me.

My customer, Kimberlie, a young, dark-skinned girl in her early twenties and a certified hood rat with a little bit of weight on her was caught off guard by Nikki's remark. She whirled herself around in my service chair and said, "Now, I ain't trying to be funny, Nikki, but you need to care because if you fuck around and get me caught up in that drama that should between you and Kira, I'm gon' act like a pure fool up in here."

"Kimberlie, I'm not scared of your ghetto ass!"

"All right, Nikki, now that's enough! You are going too damn far!"

I yelled. This bitch was really going out of her damn mind and it was affecting my clients, so I felt it was time to shut her down. "Now the reason why that nigga is probably avoiding your silly ass is because I caught his trifling ass fucking the hell out of some chick in the kitchen of the nightclub! I saw it on the security monitor in Fatu's office that very same day you came up in here bragging about how good he fucked you the night before."

Nikki's eyes bugged out and her mouth fell wide open. "You saw him doing what?" she asked.

"I said, I saw his trifling ass fucking some chick in the kitchen part of the nightclub on Fatu's security camera," I repeated. "And to make matters worse, the nigga was digging her stinking ass without a damn condom."

"Oh, now that's nasty," Rachael commented from her station.

"It sure was! That's why I went off on Fatu's ass and told him to go straighten that shit out," I lied to make her stupid ass look sillier than she'd already looked. "But here you are, trying to accuse me of throwing salt when all I did was take up for you," I continued, hoping she'd drop the subject and leave me the fuck alone.

Nikki shook her head. "I don't believe that."

"What don't you believe?"

"I don't believe you saw him fucking some chick at the club. You're just talking shit so I won't fuck with him anymore. But you need to come a little harder than that, sweetheart, because I ain't gonna feed into that bullshit!"

"You know what, Nikki? I could care less whether you believe me or not. It really doesn't matter. But I'll tell you this. If you ever fuck him again, you'd better make him strap up before you fuck around and catch something you ain't gonna be able to get rid of."

"Thanks, but I don't need your advice. Keep that shit for yourself!"

I shook my head and watched her as she grabbed her handbag from the bottom drawer of her station and stormed out the door.

Rachael could not wait to open up her big-ass mouth. "What in the hell was her beef? I mean, because she was going off on you."

"Yeah, she was, but she stopped in her damn tracks! Trust me, she ain't trying to run up on me, for real! She's just upset because that nigga of hers done fucked her and played her dumb ass!"

Rachael looked around nervously. "You better not say that too loud, because you know she's got ears all over the place."

"Rachael, I wouldn't give a damn what she's got. This is my shop! I know one thing, though. She'd better not ever walk up on me and disrespect me, or any of my clients again, because the next time I'm not going to be so civil. And after I whip her ass, I'm gonna have the paramedics escort her dumb ass out of here on a stretcher."

Rachael and Kimberlie both burst into laughter. "Damn, that would be a sight to see," Kimberlie said.

"You ain't lying about that," Rachael agreed.

The other clients chuckled and nodded their heads in agreement. Two hours of nonstop services to my clients passed before I was able to put my last client under the dryer and take a break. "I'm going out for a bite to eat. Does anybody want anything while I'm out?" I asked while I was getting my handbag and car keys.

"Where are you going?" Rachael wanted to know.

"Probably to the Chinese restaurant around the corner."

"Well, bring me four spring rolls and a lot of duck sauce."

"All right," I replied and left.

While I walked to my car I noticed Nikki standing beside her car, talking to Sophie's husband. She was smiling her ass off too. If I had to guess what they were talking about, it would be that he was trying to convince her to go out with him and possibly give him some pussy afterward. Judging from how fast she jumped in bed with that other African nigga Bintu, it wouldn't surprise me if she sneaked off and went to a hotel with Sophie's husband that night. That was just how trifling she'd gotten lately. All I could do was shake my head, because she needed some help with her self-esteem issues. Not only that, I knew that if Sophie decided to walk out of her shop and saw her husband grinning all up in Nikki's face, she would go upside both of their fucking heads. It wouldn't be shit Nikki could do to stop her either, because Sophie was a big bitch! The ho looked like she could fuck up her husband with those big-ass hands and feet she had, so Nikki better watch out because I knew she was not trying to get her Anna Sui halter dress ripped from her body. That would be a sight to see, though, and I would laugh my ass off.

I made a couple more wisecracks about them to myself, got in my car, and got the hell out of Dodge. I figured if a fight did cap off while I was gone, Rachael would fill me in and perhaps record it on her cell phone so I could see it later. I knew that sounded really bad on my part, but, hey, what could I say, other than Nikki was gonna get everything she deserved because God don't like ugly.

On Some New Shit

(Nikki Speaks)

It had been a total of five days since I had last seen or talked to Bintu, and I hadn't spoken to that cat named Neeko until today. I started not to answer my phone when it initially rang, but when I looked down at the CallerID, I was really eager to find out what rock his ass climbed up from under. "What happened to you?" I asked instead of saying hello. "I thought you fell off the face of the earth."

"Ahhh, baby," he began to say, "I am so sorry, but a lot of shit went down after I got off the phone with you that night. Me and my peoples had to straighten some niggas who were bringing heat to our spot."

"Join the club. Because a lot of shit went down with me too."

"Trust me, your shit could not have been no worse than mine."

"If you didn't have cats pointing guns in your face and robbing you for all your shit, then you are absolutely wrong on this one."

Shocked, Neeko said, "What the fuck? Wait a minute," he continued, like he was trying to gather his thoughts, "you got robbed?"

"Yeah."

"When?"

"Right after I got off the phone with you the other night. A couple of cats walked up in me and my cousin's shop and robbed me and my two stylists for all our dough and our jewelry."

"You got to be bullshitting me!"

"No, I'm not. And what was so fucked up about it was that we couldn't even tell the police how the niggas looked."

"You didn't get to see how they looked?"

"How could we when they were wearing masks?"

"Come on now, I know they had something distinctive about them that you could've told the police."

"Neeko, whoever those niggas were, they had their shit mapped out to a T. I mean, they were covered from head to toe and they never slipped up and said either one of their names. So we had nothing to go with, and I'm frustrated like hell because I want my shit back."

"What did they take?"

"They took my seven-thousand-dollar diamond necklace, my Rolex watch, and a pair of diamond studded earrings I had just got. But my girl Carmen had the most shit of us all. That forty-thousand-dollar diamond chain she had around her neck belonged to her fiancé, so he was pissed, and then on top of that they took her five-carat diamond engagement ring he had just given her."

"Word!" he said as if he couldn't believe what he had heard.

"Neeko, you just don't know what I've been through. But what's even worse is that I ain't gonna be able to do anything about it."

"I'm sorry to hear that, baby. I mean, I wish there was something I could do to get your shit back."

"I wish you could do something too. But since you can't just keep your ears to the street and let me know if you hear something. That way if you find out who was behind it I can plug Carmen's fiancé X with the information so he can make those niggas pay."

"Are you talking about Xavier from Lincoln Park on the Northeast side?"

"I'm not sure where he's from."

"How does he look?"

"He's an average looking big guy with a bald head. Why, you know him or something?"

Neeko hesitated for a second and then he said, "I don't know him personally. But I've seen him around the way. It's a small world, huh?"

"If that's the way you want to look at it," I replied nonchalantly, so he switched the subject.

"So, what's up with me and you? When we gon' hang out?"

"It's up to you. You're the one with the woman and a hectic schedule."

Neeko laughed. "It ain't like that for real."

"Well, I guess you can answer that question yourself."

"I'm free any day of the week."

"What about tonight? You trying to go out and get a bite to eat?"

"Yeah, we can do that. But what time are you talking about?"

"Let's meet up about seven-thirty."

"A'ight. But where we gon' meet at?"

"Do you remember where I told you my shop was?"

"Yeah."

"Well, meet me there."

"A'ight," he said and then we hung up.

A while later Neeko called my cell phone and told me he was parked outside, so I grabbed my handbag and hauled ass outside. Rachael was the only one left in the shop servicing her last client, so I mentioned that I was about to leave right after I got my phone call.

"Whatcha' doing tonight? Going home to relax?"

I smiled. "No ma'am, I am about to go on a hot date with my new friend waiting for me outside."

"Who is he? And when did you meet him?"

"His name is Neeko and I met him about a week ago while I was getting me some lunch from Quiznos."

"Is he cute?"

"Hell yeah!"

"What does he drive?"

"A Yukon Denali."

"Wow! Sounds like you got a winner."

"Too soon to tell, but I shall find out," I said and then I grabbed the doorknob and let myself out.

"Be careful," I heard her yell before the door closed.

On my way to Neeko's truck I noticed that he was yelling at someone on the other end of his cell phone, so I took about six steps toward the passenger side door and then I turned my back to him so he could have some privacy. I acted like I was looking inside the bakery shop next to the salon, but I was really ear-hustling my ass off. Whoever he was talking to, he was chewing his ass out.

"Nigga, do you know who the fuck I am? I will kill you and your whole fucking family!" I heard him say and then he got quiet as if he was giving the caller a chance to speak. "Well, nigga, if you think you got enough fighting power, bring that shit to me!" I heard him scream and then he abruptly ended the call.

Now I couldn't tell you who the hell he was beefing with or what it was about, but I did know that Neeko was furious, and if anybody tried to cross him right then, I was sure he'd take care of their ass real good, and I sure wouldn't want to be nowhere around to witness it.

Several seconds later he honked his horn and gestured for me to hop into his whip, so I did. Immediately after I sat in the seat next to him he smiled and said, "Nice to finally see you after all this time."

I cracked a cute little smile. "It's your fault."

"Yeah, I know. That's why I'm going to make it up to you." He pulled off and headed northwest.

"Where we going?" I asked.

"I gotta make a quick run to pick up some dough, and then we can go get something to eat."

"Where you want to get something to eat at?"

"It's up to you."

I pulled out my Blackberry to make a quick call. "Good," I said, "because I've been dying to get a bite to eat at Benihana this entire week."

"You like their food?"

"Oh my God! I love it! Why, you don't like it?"

"I've only been there one time and it was a'ight."

"Which one did you go to?"

"The one on Louisiana Street."

"That's the one I go to. Their food is always fresh. I love it and I'm getting ready to call there right now and make us a reservation."

"Damn, you got them on speed dial, huh?"

I chuckled. "I sure do," I said, and then I started speaking into the phone.

After I made the reservation, I sat back in the seat and made small talk with Neeko while he made his way to his destination. Everything was going according to plan. He was looking good and being a gentleman. He also threw out a few jokes every now and again to make me laugh, and I was truly enjoying his company.

About ten minutes into the drive his cell phone started ringing again, so he looked at the CallerID to see who it was. When he didn't recognize the number, he said, "Who the fuck is this?"

I looked at him, but said nothing. He kept staring at it, hesitating to answer it. Then at the last minute, he decided to see who it was. "Hello," he finally said.

"Where you at?" I heard a woman's voice yell through the receiver.

Irritated by her tone, he said, "I'm taking care of business. Where you at? And whose phone you calling me from?"

From the looks of his conversation, I knew it had to be his woman. I didn't care, though, because I was with him at the moment and I had big plans to spend some of that money he was about to pick up.

"Look, I ain't trying to argue with you right now, so I'ma holler at you when I come to the crib," he told her and then hung up.

I cracked another smile at him and said, "Trouble at home?"

He sighed and said, "She's always bitching at me about something. She ain't never satisfied about shit! She lucky she got my son, because I would've left her ass a long time ago."

Now I saw that he was dealing with one of those baby mama drama issues, I made it my business not to make one comment. Instead, I said, "Lighten up! It's not that bad!"

Before he could say one word, his phone rang again. Without looking at the CallerID this time, he just answered it. "What?!" he lashed out.

Caught off guard by whatever the caller had just said, his mouth fell wide open and his eyeballs nearly popped out of his head. Then in slow motion, he turned around to his left. I turned with him and saw an old, beat up Chevy Impala riding side by side with him with two men pointing machine guns directly at him. Immediately both men started ripping Neeko's truck to shreds with their artillery.

Pop! Pop! Pop! Pop! Pop! Pop! Pop! Pop! Pop! Bullets were flying through doors and shattering the windows and all I could do was scream and duck for cover. After Neeko got hit, he dropped his phone to the floor and let out a loud grunt. His facial expression was that of a man who was in excruciating pain and I wanted no part of it. My first reaction was to help him get us the hell away from these guys before we were both dead. I couldn't see where we were going since I was crouched down on the floor, and at this point it didn't matter since he and I had one common goal, and that was to get the hell out of Dodge. I figured since he had his hands on the wheel and his eyes on the road all I needed to do was give him some help with the accelerator since he wasn't going fast enough for me.

I reached over and pressed my hand down on his right foot as hard as I could until I felt his truck move faster. I could feel the truck swerving like crazy, and the only thought that crossed my mind was that we were about to lose our lives and I couldn't let that happen. I had a lot to live for, and besides, I had just met this nigga. He and I had no history together and we hadn't even fucked each other, so I was not about to go out on a limb with him.

My heart was racing like crazy while the bullets continued to find their way through the left side of Neeko's truck. All I could hear was popping sounds and Neeko screaming like a bitch, yelling at the people in front of him to get out of the way. I ain't gon' lie, I was screaming my ass off too. Shit, I wanted to get the hell away from those psycho-ass niggas, but the way things were looking, Neeko acted like he couldn't shake them for nothing in the world. He was racing down the highway going at a speed of about 120 miles per hour, dipping in and out of lanes, but those niggas were still gunning at him real hard.

"Ahhh shit! These niggas are busting shots at my gas tank. They trying to blow us the fuck up!" Neeko said, panicking.

"Go! Go! Go!" I yelled and immediately forced my arm through the small space where the accelerator was and pressed down on it as hard as I could. The engine revved and I knew Neeko's adrenaline must have been pumping. But it seemed like we couldn't shake those niggas for nothing in this world.

Still down on the floor, I could hear the other cars swerving and stomping on brakes to try to get out of our way, but for the life of me, I couldn't figure out why I hadn't heard the sirens of a police squad car. We'd been racing down this highway preventing those niggas in the next car from killing us for the past three to four minutes and no one had come to our rescue. What type of place was this? I knew that if we were in Virginia, the police would've showed up sixty seconds after the first shot was fired.

I buried my face between my arms and started praying. But as soon as I got to the part where I was asking God to spare my life, Neeko's truck came to a screeching halt. *BOOM!* The impact of the crash shook me like a rattle. When I looked up, I noticed that both airbags had deployed. The passenger side airbag was sticking out like a white balloon, and Neeko's face was buried deep in the airbag, which had knocked him unconscious.

I scrambled to my feet and pushed my way past the passenger's side airbag to get into the seat. Once I was all the way up, I was able to look outside, and that was when I noticed that we had crashed into a metal rail on an exit ramp. When I realized where I was and that Neeko's truck was smashed up really badly in the front, I knew that the police would surely be on their way. If I was caught with this guy, I was going to have to answer a lot of questions. And that would lead to my probation officer finding out what kind of niggas I was getting involved with, and I couldn't have that, so I grabbed my handbag, pushed the passenger side door open, and hopped out of the truck.

I saw a lot of cars ride by the truck slowly to see what condition we were in, but I wasn't paying their asses any mind. My main objective was to get the hell out of there. While I was walking away from the scene, this white man approached me while I stumbled across the grass and onto the pavement.

"Are you OK?" he asked, reaching out to grab my arm.

I snatched my arm away from him and gave him a mean look. "Yes, I'm fine. Now please move out of my damn way."

"I was only trying to help you," the man explained. But I wasn't trying to hear him. My main concern was to get the hell out of there before the police came, so I kept my head down the entire time to prevent the man from getting a good look at me so he couldn't give the police a good description.

Getting caught up in more bullshit with these nothing-ass niggas was becoming a bit tiresome. Thank God I didn't get hurt, because that would have meant a ride to the hospital with the paramedics and a three-hundred-fifty-dollar tab for carrying me there on a stretcher. Besides that, my probation officer was a beast, so I couldn't give that ho any reason to violate me. And the shit that just went on would be just the right amount of ammunition to have my ass cornered in her office answering a whole lot of questions. I was not in the mood for that, so I was gonna flag down the next taxi I saw and make my way back to my car.

I walked down the ramp that led to a busy intersection and at that intersection I saw a slew of cabs going in all directions, so I put my best foot forward and got into the first one that stopped. "Take me to the uptown district," I instructed the driver.

"Where exactly are you trying to go?"

"Smith Street," I told him and then I sat back in the seat.

The entire drive all I could think about was how badly Neeko was hurt. I knew he wasn't dead because when I checked his wrist for a pulse, he was still breathing. I wasn't a medical expert, but I knew that he had to be in real bad shape from all those gunshot wounds. But thankfully enough, I didn't witness him getting killed. And I didn't plan on seeing it happen on another date, so as far as I was concerned, that nigga was history. I was changing my number and crossing my fingers that he didn't try to contact me anymore.

After the cab driver dropped me off at my destination, I hopped into my vehicle and left from downtown in a split second. I was doing forty miles per hour down Main Street and I didn't have the slightest idea where I was going. I didn't want to go home because I knew Kira was there and I wasn't in the mood to see her. And I didn't want to go back to the shop because Rachael's nosey ass would have a lot of questions for me. And who knew, the police could have come up there looking for me too, especially if Neeko was one of those snitching type of niggas. So what was I going to do?

Depressed about my bad luck with these nothing ass niggas, I decided to hop on the phone and see if I could catch Bintu. I needed someone to vent to about what I had just gone through. I thought he might feel sorry for me and want to see me so he could console me, and that was just what I needed. I dialed his number and let it ring until it went to voice mail. I refused to leave a voice mail because I hated talking into those stupid things, so I got up the nerve to ride up to his nightclub. Shit, at that point I really didn't care how he was going to take the fact that I had just popped up on him. I needed to talk, and he was the only man I could think of who I could confide in. I mean, he at least owed me that much since he'd been avoiding me.

Just a couple days ago I had gone to club looking for him, but I hadn't been able to catch his ass. Fatu had lied to me and told me that Bintu had left town to take care of some business, and that he'd be gone for at least another week, but I didn't buy that bullshit-ass lie. I was from Missouri, which was the Show Me state, so I had to see if he was in town for myself.

This time I decided to camp out in my car outside the nightclub. After about three long hours of waiting around, I started getting impatient and decided that I should go inside. Just when I was about to get out of my car Bintu strolled outside with some bimbo attached to his arm.

"I knew that nigga wasn't out of town!" I screamed at the top of my voice, punching the steering wheel as hard as I could, but at the same time avoiding the pad that would have set off my car horn. Accidentally hitting my car horn would have blown up my whole plan of catching this nigga off guard.

As I emerged from my car, I was able to get a better look at this bitch he had dangling from his arm, and from what I saw, she wasn't even all that! I could also see that they were both drunk because they were stumbling all over each other. They were carrying on like two alcoholics in fucking heat. Bintu was feeling all over this chick like he wanted to fuck her smack dab in the middle of the sidewalk.

The more I watched, the more my blood pressure went up, so talking to him about the shootout I was in with Neeko went right out the window. Without much thought, I jumped out of my car and stormed toward them like a raging bull. I had nothing else on my mind but to whip her ass and kick Bintu in his fucking balls. I wanted both of them to see how it felt to be hurt.

"You're getting ready to take her to your house so you can fuck her, just like you did me the other night, huh?" I roared.

Stunned by the way I had just come out of nowhere, the woman staggered a little bit, trying to keep her balance. Bintu just stood there like he'd seen a ghost. I marched straight toward them, pushed the woman down to the ground, and immediately started throwing blows at Bintu. "Nigga, you ain't shit! Got me 'round here calling you, leaving you messages, and you ain't got the decency to call me back to let me know what's up with us!" I screamed while I pounded the hell out of his head.

Bintu tried desperately to shield his head with his arms. He managed to say, "What's your damn problem? Why are you acting like this?"

"Nigga, don't play stupid! You had me lying in your bed, sucking on your little-ass dick and pretended like we were going to be together. You knew you weren't trying to be in a relationship with me, so why did you play with my damn feelings?" I continued to pound him as tears fell from my eyes. "I am so sick of niggas like you carrying me like I'm some tramp or something. I am not a slut, so stop treating me like one!"

"What's going on?" I heard a man yell from the front of the club.

I ignored his ass and continued to send down my wrath upon Bintu. Right when I was getting the best of his drunken ass, one of Bintu's cousins grabbed me from behind and swung my ass around like I was a fucking rag doll. I didn't know what hit me when I was flung to the ground. I scraped my knees and hands up pretty badly, but that didn't stop me from getting back to my feet. I came back up swinging even harder.

"What's wrong with you, nigga? You ain't got no business putting your motherfucking hands on me!" I screamed.

The cousin had his back turned to me, trying to make sure Bintu was OK, so I charged at both of them. My punches landed on the cousin's back and he retaliated quickly by putting me in a chokehold. I couldn't breathe to save my life. Luckily for me, the nigga was only trying to restrain me from attacking them, because if he was trying to kill me, I would have been dead thirty seconds ago. Struggling to regain control of the situation, I kicked and squirmed the entire time he held me.

Finally a voice registered in my head. It was Fatu, and boy was I glad to see him!

"What's wrong with you, Kofi? You're not supposed to be handling a woman like that," he said, chastising his cousin. Fatu turned to me.

"Are you OK?" he asked.

Trying to regain my composure, I took a deep breath and massaged my neck. I nodded in response to his question. He turned back to Kofi and asked him why he had me in a headlock.

"She was hitting me and Bintu in our backs, so I had to stop her," Kofi began to explain.

"You didn't have to choke the hell out of me," I croaked.

"If you'd kept your hands to yourself, I would not have had to put my hands on you."

"Oh, go to hell!" I spat.

"What's going on?" Fatu asked.

"She came from out of nowhere and started attacking us," the woman blurted out.

"Bitch, I didn't touch you!" I pointed out.

"You pushed me on the ground!"

"You lucky I didn't go upside your fucking head!"

Bintu stood alongside the nightclub with his back posted up against the wall. He wouldn't say a word. It was apparent he was pretty out of it from all the alcohol he had, not to mention I'd popped him pretty badly. From the looks of it, I'd stung him real good in his right eye and I was happy as hell because of it. I bet he wouldn't play with my feelings anymore.

"Look, Nikki, I know you're upset, but we can't have this type of thing going on here outside the club."

"Fatu, you know I've been trying to get in touch with Bintu for the longest. So when I saw him coming out of the club with this bitch all over him, I snapped. I mean, it was like he totally forgot about me." I began to sob.

Fatu took my arm and escorted me to my car. I resisted at first because I wanted to talk to Bintu. I wanted him to look me in my face and tell me why he did me the way he did. I mean, that was the least he could have done. I felt like I deserved at least that much, but when Fatu explained to me that right then wasn't a good time to approach Bintu because I probably would not get a straight answer out of him while the other woman was present, not to mention the fact that he was a bit drunk, I nodded and proceeded to my car.

"When am I gonna be able to talk to him? You know now he's really gonna avoid me after what just happened."

"Don't worry about tonight. I'm going to talk to him. Everything is going to be fine."

"Well, would you call me and let me know how everything went?"

"I'll tell you what,"—He got silent, as if he went into deep thought—"why don't you call me tomorrow afternoon?"

"I don't have your number," I said.

Fatu gave me his cell phone number and then we parted ways. I noticed Bintu had walked back into the club and Kofi was ushering Bintu's whore into a cab. I was very pleased to see her carry her ass home. At least she and Bintu wouldn't be spending the night together, so I felt like something did end in my favor.

On my way back to the house, I called Fatu and told him the main reason why I acted out like I did. He was sympathetic when I told him about the accident I had with Neeko, which made me feel good because I finally had someone to share it with. After I spilled my beans, I made him promise not to tell Kira about last night and about what I had just told him. He promised me that he wouldn't, so I was happy about that. Before we hung up he reminded me to call him the next day.

"I will," I promised.

The following day while Kira and I were at work, I slipped outside and called Fatu. I had to make sure she was busy working on a client so she couldn't eavesdrop on my call. My heart was beating really fast because I had no idea what he was going to tell me about Bintu. When Fatu answered the phone, I exhaled and waited to hear what he had to say.

"Are you all right?" he asked.

"Yes, I'm fine. But how is Bintu?"

"He's doing OK. Not too pleased about how you attacked him, but other than that, he's fine."

"Did you get to talk to him?"

"Yes, we spoke about what happened."

"What did he say? Why was he avoiding me?"

Fatu hesitated for a moment and then he said, "First off, he said he wasn't avoiding you. Secondly, he did say that you are a beautiful woman, but you and him aren't on the same page, and that you two have different views about a lot of things, so he saw no need to lead you on."

"Where is he now? I want to talk to him," I snapped.

"He's at our apartment, resting."

I sighed heavily. "Fatu, that lame-ass excuse he gave you was bullshit, and you know it. I mean, let's be real! He knows damn well he played me for a one-night stand. So why won't he just 'fess up to it and stop being a fucking pussy about it!"

"Calm down, Nikki."

"Come on now, Fatu, let's be real! How in the hell is it humanly possible for a woman to calm down after she gets fucked one night, and the nigga who fucked her will not return her call the very next day? That's some devastating shit, especially when the dick wasn't that good. Did you know that I had to suck him off to get his dick hard so he could fuck me? That was a lot of damn work and I didn't even get paid for it, so my feelings are hurt!"

"I'm sorry about all of this."

"You don't have to apologize. It wasn't your fault. I'm the one who allowed this cat to play me, even though I had reservations about it. But let me ask you this."

"What is it?"

"Was it true that Kira caught him fucking some chick in the kitchen area of the club?"

"What did Bintu say?"

"I didn't get the chance to ask him. Remember? He's been avoiding me."

"Wait a minute, how did you find out about that?"

"Come on now, you know who told me. And anyway, that's not important. What is important is why he's avoiding me."

"Stop staying that. He's not avoiding you."

"Easy for you to say when you're not the one 'round here with your heart all fucked up."

"What are you doing right now?"

"I'm standing outside the salon."

"Where's Kira?"

"She's inside doing a client's hair."

"Would you like to meet me for lunch so we can continue to talk about this?"

"Sure. But where?"

"Come down to the Oceanaire Seafood Room at the Galleria."

"What time?"

"Come now," he insisted.

"All right."

I went back inside the shop to retrieve my handbag. I told both Kira and Rachael that I had to make a quick run. Thank God no one asked me where I was off to, so I was out of there in a jiffy.

While I drove to the restaurant I laughed at the thought that I was on my way to have lunch with Kira's man. She would have a fit if she knew! Now that I thought about it, I might use this secret lunch date to blow her mind on a later date if she pissed me off. She had a fucking field day with the fact that she caught Bintu fucking some chick in the kitchen area of the nightclub, so I would love to get her ass back. The expression on her face would be priceless, and I knew that I would laugh my ass off. That was a piece of payback that I would love to dish out.

When I finally arrived at the restaurant I had to wait an additional fifteen minutes before Fatu joined me. He was looking really good dressed in his Burberry denim jeans and a Burberry polo to match. I thought it was really cute seeing him dressed casual since I'd always seen him sporting expensive Armani silk and linen suits. He smiled at me as he approached the table, so I stood to greet him. When we embraced one another the touch of his arms and hands were like magic. And the cologne he wore was out of this world. The fragrance was soft but masculine. It took my breath away.

"What is that you're wearing?" I asked.

"It's Marc Jacobs," he told me and immediately took his seat.

I took my seat too and admired him from where I was. Deep down inside I wanted to hop right on his lap and give him a big fat kiss, but I decided against it. Didn't want to scare him off.

"I have something for you," he said and pulled a small jewelry box from his right jean pocket.

My eyes grew three inches bigger. "Oh my God! What is it?" I asked as I took the box from his hand.

He sat back and remained silent while I opened the box. After I saw what was inside my mouth fell wide open.

"Fatu, it's beautiful!" I said, admiring the fourteen-karat gold women's Presidential Rolex watch.

"I'm glad you like it," he replied.

"What is this for?" I asked while I was detaching the watch from the plastic packaging it was wrapped around.

"For your troubles," he said. "I'm sorry about my brother. Here, let me put it on for you," he continued as he took the watch out of my hand. While he was fastening the links together, I couldn't help but wonder why fate didn't leave me and him to hook up. I could've been the best thing he ever had.

"There you go," he said after he straightened my watch.

I took another look at it and smiled my ass off. "Damn, this is nice! No one has ever given me anything like this before."

"Well, they should have."

"Be honest. Did this come from Bintu?"

"No. It's a gift from me."

I smiled. "You are so sweet!"

He smiled back. "Believe me, I'm not this way all the time."

"I'm sure. But I need to know how I can pay you back. I mean, I know this Rolex had to set you back at least ten grand."

"You're close," he said.

"Are you serious?"

"I don't like to talk about money, so let's just figure out what we're going to eat," he said, cutting me off.

"OK, but will you at least tell me what I can do to repay you?"

He placed his menu down and said, "Don't worry about it. It was a gift."

"I understand. But I feel like I've got to do something for you. That's just how I roll. So can you please give me a chance to show you how much I appreciate you giving me this?"

Fatu thought for a second and then he said, "OK, I'll tell you what, when I think of something, I'll let you know."

"And I will be ready," I assured him and then I looked back at my watch.

The watch was nice as hell. Fatu really knew how to pick out expensive gifts. The only fucked-up thing about it was that it was probably the last time this nigga would cop a gift like that for me. I had to savor that moment for the rest of my life, because I remembered he was involved with Kira. But if she ever fucked up, I was going to be on the sidelines waiting to scoop him right on up.

"I appreciate you taking out the time to have lunch with me so we can talk," I said as I played with my watch.

"Nikki, you're a beautiful girl, so that's the least I can do."

"Can I ask you a question?"

"Sure."

"When you first saw me at the gas station, was I attractive to you then?"

"Yes, you were."

"OK, well why didn't you try to talk to me first?"

Caught off guard by my question, he hesitated for a moment and then he said, "I'm sorry, but I don't know how to answer that."

"Well, try as best as you can, because I'm curious. I mean, you and I probably would have made a good couple." I pressed the issue.

"You think so?" He smiled.

"I know so."

Still apparently at a loss for words, Fatu just sat there twiddling his thumbs. He must've thought that I was trying to set him up or something because he would not open his mouth for nothing in the world. I reached across the table and massaged his hands. "Look, I'm sorry for putting you on the spot, but I got to know why you didn't try to hook up with me first."

"I really can't say," he said, and then paused for a second before continuing. "I remember pulling up and Bintu making references about introducing himself to you, so I sat back and let him go for it."

I shook my head. "Oh my God! I can't believe this," I said. "Do you know that when y'all pulled up that night, I had my eyes set on you? I was furious when Bintu approached me," I lied to see how he'd react.

"Really?"

"Hell yeah! I was attracted to you."

"Why didn't you say something?"

"What was I supposed to say?"

Before Fatu could respond to my question our waitress came to our table, took our drink orders, and then she left, giving us a few more minutes to decide what we wanted to order. While we were looking over our menu I watched Fatu's body language through my peripheral vision. He seemed like he was feeling a little uneasy, so I said, "Am I making you feel awkward?"

"No, I'm fine," he said. But I knew he was lying. Mixed emotions were plastered all over his face.

I grabbed his hands again and said, "Look, I am so sorry for bringing all of this up. But I just had to tell you. I mean, I was feeling you from day one, and when you asked if my cousin was available, I was upset."

"Really?"

"Hell yeah!"

"But why?"

"There was just something about you. You seemed laid back and quick. And I like those type of men. They make me wonder a lot and that is so sexy to me."

Fatu smiled as if he was embarrassed. "I don't know what to say."

"You don't have to say anything. I just needed to get all of that off my shoulders, and now that I've done that, I feel like a load has been lifted."

"Well, I'm glad," he replied and then he picked up his menu.

After we finally figured out what we were going to eat, we gave the waitress our order and she was back with it less than fifteen minutes later. While we were eating, I told Fatu how my relationship with Kira was deteriorating. Then I decided to see how he would react if I told him everything I knew about Kira. I explained that she was a money grubbing whore. I also told him how much of a ride-or-die chick I was to Kira's husband, and how he hung me out to dry.

"What happened?" he asked.

"He was a big-time drug dealer and he needed someone to transport some of the work to his drug houses, so I took the job. But after about a few months, somebody tipped off the police and had me busted. So when I called him to bail me out, he basically told me to kiss his ass!"

"And what did you do?"

"I didn't do anything," I lied. "I just sat back and did my time. I'm not into that snitching shit! That's for suckers!" I continued, trying to keep a straight face.

"What did Kira do?"

"She couldn't do anything. Her hands were tied too."

"How much time did they give you?"

"Well, since I was a first-time offender and the police only caught me with two ounces of coke, I received a very light sentence of two years. All of it was suspended except six months, and now I'm on probation."

"Where is Kira's husband now?"

"Don't tell her I told you any of this, but he's dead."

"How?"

"He was murdered."

"By whom?"

"No one knows."

"Wow, that's interesting," he said and then he took a forkful of his food.

I watched him as he ate for the next three or four minutes. I had to break the ice. "Are you OK?" I asked. "I'm not scaring you off with my past life, am I?"

"No, I'm just amazed at how resilient you are. You put your life on the line for someone, lost your freedom for it, and you did not once roll over on them. That right there shows major character on your part."

Hearing Fatu praise me for some shit I didn't do put a huge smile on my face. I felt deep down inside that I was winning him over and making him regret that he hadn't stepped to me first.

After we ate he escorted me to my car and then we both parted ways. Before we parted, I kissed him on his cheek and thanked him once again for my watch.

"Don't forget I owe you one," I told him.

He smiled. "I won't."

Back at the shop I flashed my watch around so that everyone could see it. Kira didn't say a word, but I knew her hating ass got a good look at it. Rachael wanted me to spill my guts about where I had gotten it from, but I kept my lips sealed. I wasn't ready to break the news yet. I figured I'd use that ammunition for a later date.

I'm Still Wifey Material
(Kira Speaks)

Today made three months since Fatu and I had been dating. Things were really looking good for us, and I was enjoying every last bit of our romance. Today he picked me up from my house and whisked me off for a full day of shopping and pampering at the Pelican Spa. We had a ton of fun, especially when he took me back to the Aquarium restaurant, which was where we had our very first date. I had the Thai marinated fish with crab legs and a house salad, while Fatu had the blackened tuna and a few items from their tapas menu. The evening was beautiful and the ambiance was on point. What really set off the night was when Fatu reached into his pants pocket and pulled out a black jewelry box. My face lit up.

"Oh, my God! What is this?" I asked.

He opened the box and turned it around toward me. "Will you marry me?" he asked, revealing a gigantic emerald cut, canary-colored diamond inside a platinum setting.

That diamond had to be at least eight or nine carats, if not more. I tried desperately not to jump out of my chair from excitement. Instead I politely smiled and said, "Yes."

Fatu slid the ring onto my finger and then he kissed my hand. "You know what this means, right?"

Confused by the question, I said, "No, I don't."

He held my hand with a firm grip and said, "This means that you and I are engaged now. You are officially my fiancée."

I smiled at the sound of that, because it sounded really good. But then I started thinking about how we had only known each other for three months, so we might have been taking things a little too fast.

"Honey, do you think we're taking this thing a little too fast?" I asked Fatu.

"No, I don't. I'm in love with you, and I don't think we should put a time limit on that."

"I feel the same way, but I don't want to mess up what we have by rushing into something we might regret later."

"Don't speak like that. I am a firm believer that the way you go into a relationship is the way it is going to end. Haven't things been going really good for us? Aren't you happy when you're with me?"

"Yes, everything is going really well for us, and of course I'm happy when I'm with you. But I just want us to take this thing one day at a time so we won't run into any misunderstandings."

"Baby, I understand all of that, but we're not going to have any problems. My love for you is solid. And I don't want to wait a long time for you to be Mrs. Fatu Oduka."

The words coming from his mouth were magical and breathtaking. I was literally about to melt. What man do you know who pours out his heart like that and sounds like he means it? Fatu had convinced me that we didn't necessarily have to have a long engagement before we tied the knot, so I said, "So when do you think we should get married?"

"Well, I was hoping we could do it on New Year's Day."

"Oh my God, Fatu! New Year's is only six months away!"

He smiled. "I know. So what do you think?"

I smiled back at him and said, "That's fine. We can do it."

He raced around the table to me and kissed me dead on the mouth. He was very passionate and he made my pussy wet too. I talked him into paying the check so we could get out of there. I wanted to go straight to his place so we could fuck the hell out of each other.

Before we left he handed me an envelope. I opened it and found a deposit slip in it from an offshore bank account with my name on it. I was even more speechless when I saw all the dough he had in that account. "When did you do this?" I asked.

"Just this morning."

"This is a lot of money," I said, looking at all the zeros behind the number one.

"It's all for you. I want to make sure you are OK just in case anything ever happens to me."

"Nothing is going to ever happen to you," I assured him and hugged him for dear life.

Back at his place we wasted little time hopping into the sack. After we sucked and fucked each other, I lay back in the bed and admired my ring while he was asleep. I knew a little bit about what to look for in a diamond as far as clarity was concerned, so I turned that joint inside out, trying to see what I was working with. I knew when I got home Nikki was going to have something to say, so I was prepared. More than likely, she was going to have something negative to say because she was a fucking hater. But I wasn't gonna pay her silly ass no mind. My mission, from this point on, was to get a wedding planner so my new fiancé and I could get our show on the road.

Since I was in such a good mood the next morning, I got up and cooked my man a couple of Belgium waffles and some turkey link sausages. Fatu smiled when he came into the kitchen and saw me half dressed, wearing only an apron.

"I love seeing you dressed like that. You look very sexy."

I smiled and placed his plate in front of him. "Thank you, baby." I gave him a wet one on the lips. "How did you sleep last night?"

"I slept very well. And you?"

"Baby, I ain't gonna lie, I couldn't get a drop of sleep last night."

"Why not?"

"Because I couldn't keep my eyes off this ring. Baby, it's so beautiful! I know you must've paid at least ten grand for it." I hoped he'd tell me exactly how much he had dropped on it.

"Let's just say that you could trade that ring in, buy two of the same model Lexuses that you drive now, and you'd still have money left over."

My eyes grew two inches bigger. "Come on, now. You're joking, right?" I wanted just a little more clarification. If I'd just heard him correctly, he told me that my ring was worth one hundred forty thousand dollars plus tax, since my Lexus cost me seventy thousand. If I had calculated this right, Fatu paid over one hundred fifty thousand dollars for my engagement ring. That was some major shit.

"No, I'm not kidding," he assured me. "But look at it this way. You are worth every penny."

I kissed him on his forehead. "You're so sweet!" I said as I passed him the bottle of syrup.

He drizzled a modest amount of syrup over his waffle and dug right into it. Once I made myself a plate of food, I sat down at the table beside him. We talked about everything under the sun, but most importantly, we discussed the colors we were going to wear for our wedding. After we decided to incorporate pearl white, platinum, and gray, we got to the subject about what our living arrangements were going to be after the wedding. Fatu first suggested that I come live with him at his place, but I wasn't feeling that idea, so I made the suggestion that we buy a new home, somewhere we could have a big backyard for the children we were gonna have. He thought that would be a good idea and told me he was going to have his Realtor look into it for us.

I got really excited by the idea of getting a bigger home, a place where we could raise our children. I could tell that Fatu was excited about it too, because after he finished his food, he got right on the phone and called his real estate agent. He spoke to her briefly and then he handed me the phone so I could tell her exactly how many bedrooms and bathrooms I wanted, along with the amenities I was looking for. She wrote down every one of my requests and told me she'd get back with me in a few days. I told her to take her time because we weren't in a rush. She congratulated me on our engagement, and then we hung up.

Before I left his apartment, I messed around and gave Fatu some more pussy. That was the least I could do, considering I was sporting a one-hundred-fifty-thousand-dollar rock on my finger. There was no man in my life, prior to Fatu, who could top that. No one! I was going to hold on to him, because his type didn't come around often.

She's One Frontin'-Ass Bitch

(Nikki Speaks)

Kira strolled her silly ass in here this morning, skinning and grinning about how nice of a night she had. What really took the cake was when she walked around the kitchen doing everything she could possibly do to use her left hand, so I could see her fake-ass diamond. I knew she wanted me to ask her where she got it, but I already had an idea, so I would not give her the pleasure. Instead, I grabbed myself a bowl of cereal and headed into the living room so I could watch some TV. That tactic didn't work because she followed me there, carrying a glass of orange juice. She sat down on the sofa, facing me, and used her left hand to hold her glass. I burst into laughter because I found her actions to be so funny.

"What's so funny?" she asked.

"You," I said.

"Why am I funny?"

"I don't have to tell you. You already know."

She smiled. "Did I give it away?" She fanned her hand around, indirectly admiring her ring.

I ignored her and pretended to be engrossed in the TV.

"You know, Fatu asked me to marry him last night."

"That's nice," I commented without looking at her.

"Well, are you happy for me?"

"Kira, if you like it, I love it."

"Why are you being so nonchalant about this?"

I finally looked at her. "Because it's not my life."

"I understand all of that, but you could still be happy for me. I mean, if the shoe was on the other foot, I would be happy for you."

"Well, Kira, I'm sorry! But I am not you."

"Look, Nikki, enough with all the sarcasm! You always got to fuck up a wet dream!"

"I didn't ask you to come in here and start a conversation with me. I was sitting here with my bowl of cereal, minding my own business, and then here you come with this nonsense. Why don't you just leave me alone?"

Kira got quiet for a second, then said, "OK, I'll leave you alone, but will you help me plan my wedding in your spare time?"

"With all that money Fatu got, tell that nigga to get you a wedding planner," I shot back and continued to look at the TV.

She sat there on the sofa, looking stupid as hell. She looked like she wanted to curse my ass out, but I guess she thought about the fact that I wasn't in the mood to be fucked with, so she ended up changing her facial expression. "Will you at least be in my wedding?" she asked.

"I'll think about it."

I guess Kira couldn't take being around me any longer because she got up from the sofa and hauled ass into her room. I snickered behind her back, because I loved it when she gave me the power to push her buttons. When that happened, I won every time.

I decided not to stick around the house after my movie went off, so I got dressed and left. While I was on the road, I got a call from Carmen. This was her second time calling me since the robbery, but I knew she hadn't called Kira. Carmen and I were always closer than her and Kira.

"Whatcha doing?" she asked.

"In my car, driving to the mall."

"Whatcha getting at the mall?"

"I don't know, but I'm sure I'll find something. What are you doing?"

"Out riding around, looking for a spot to lease so I can open up my salon."

"Have you seen anywhere you'd like to be?"

"Yeah. I ran across a couple of spots, but the parking was bad, so I'm gonna keep looking until I see something."

"Well, good luck, because finding a spot with good parking is going to be hard. You know how it is around here."

"Yeah, I know. But I'm sure I'm gonna find something. Hey, listen, don't forget that I'm getting married two weekends from now."

"I haven't forgotten. Have you picked out your dress yet?"

"Yeah, girl! My dress was made right before I left the shop."

"So did you ever get another ring?"

"Of course I did! As a matter-of-fact, my baby took me to the diamond gallery and got me the exact same ring. I was happy as hell too, because I loved that ring."

"Well, I'm glad. Have you heard anything about who may have robbed us?"

"Nah, I haven't. But my baby is keeping his ears to the streets, so he's bound to find out something."

"I hope so. But guess what?"

"What?"

"Kira brought her stupid ass in the house this morning with an engagement ring on her finger."

"Whaaaaaatttttt! You kidding?"

"Nope."

"So she and that Nigerian cat is making it official, huh?"

"I guess," I responded nonchalantly.

"So how does this ring look?"

"Oh, I ain't gonna front! It's pretty as hell!"

"How many carats is it?"

"I'm not sure, but it's a canary-colored diamond, and it's big as hell."

Carmen fell silent.

"Hello, you there?" I asked.

"Yeah, I'm here. So Kira's getting married too, huh?"

"Yep."

"So what's this guy do besides own that nightclub?"

"I think he's selling drugs too, because a lot of people don't be going in there like I thought, so he has to be making money somehow."

"Really?"

"Yes, really. He's got to be doing something to keep the mortgage payments going on that apartment he's living in, not to mention that Bentley he's driving."

"Yeah, you're right. So did she say what she was going to do with her house once they get married?"

"Nah, we didn't get into it."

"Are you going to be her maid of honor?" Carmen asked before she burst into laughter.

"Hell nah! You know I don't fuck with that bitch like that!"

"Did she ask you?"

"You know she did."

"So are you at least going to her wedding?"

"Yeah, I'ma go, but when that pastor asks the question, 'Who in here feels like these two shouldn't be joined together, speak now or forever hold your peace,' I'ma jump right up."

Carmen burst into laughter again. "You ain't gonna do that."

"Watch me and see."

"What's the beef? Why you don't want them to get married?"

"Because he was supposed to be with me," I explained. "When we first met them, I was trying to talk to Fatu first, but his cousin Bintu hopped out of the damn car and beat him to the punch. To keep from being rude, I went on and had a chat with Bintu and gave him my number."

"Well, if it was like that, then I see why you're mad. But don't dwell on that mess. Go out and find yourself somebody else. You're a pretty girl, and it's plenty of niggas out here, so you ain't gon' have no problems."

"It's funny you say that, because I was kicking it with this cat named Neeko and we were supposed to go out to dinner that night we got robbed, but of course it didn't happen because of all that went on."

"Ahhh, I'm sorry to hear that."

"Oh, no, don't be sorry, because out of the fucking blue this nigga comes back on the scene and asked me to go out with him again, so I said yes."

"Where did y'all go?"

"Down the highway of hell. That nigga almost got me killed."

"Whatcha mean by that? What happened?"

"OK, like I said, I hadn't heard from him since the night before we got robbed and then he calls me out of the blue apologizing and telling me about how he got caught in some beef with some cats from out his way. So I bought into his story and jumped at the first opportunity to go out with him and that turned out to be a fucking disaster."

"What did he do?"

"That motherfucker got me caught up in a shootout. Niggas were gunning his truck down as soon as I hopped inside it."

"Oh, *that* Neeko? Oh my God! I heard about that. That shit happened not too long ago."

"Yep, it sure did."

"I can't believe you were in the car with him. That cat is straight crazy and everybody and their mama who is out there in those streets is trying to kill 'im."

"But why?"

"Because he's known for robbing motherfuckers! Or setting them up to get robbed."

"Are you kidding me?"

"Hell nah! I'm dead serious! It wouldn't surprise me if he had something to do with us getting robbed."

"You know what, Carmen, you might be right. Because now that I think about it, he asked me how business was that day, and right after I told him it was good, we hung up, and then a few seconds later, niggas were running up in the shop to rob us."

Carmen immediately changed her tone. I could tell that she had instantly gotten a bad taste in her mouth. "How did he act when he picked you up?"

"Like normal."

"That nigga thinks he's fucking slick. But he fucked with the wrong one if he had something to do with us getting robbed."

"Whatcha gon' do?"

"I'm gonna call Xavier as soon as we get off the phone so he can go out the way and ask some questions."

"I don't think that's gonna be a good idea. I mean, he should sit back and watch Neeko's moves and keep his ears to the street to see if somebody slips up."

"Fuck that! That nigga needs to be dealt with now. Shit, he's lucky he got away with just a couple of flesh wounds to his legs and arms. I know that if X's people's was on his ass while he was racing down the highway, they would've got him with one shot to the head. Plain and simple."

"Well, whatever you do, don't say I told you shit. I don't want nobody coming back to look for me."

"Oh, you ain't gotta worry about that. Xavier is going to take care of that ass and ain't nobody gonna have to worry about that nigga taking another motherfucking thing from them ever again. Speaking of which, when was the last time you spoke to Neeko?"

"I haven't spoken to him since we crashed on the side of the highway."

"Well, word is he's been trying to stay low key until all that shit blows over, but if he knows like I know, him hiding out ain't gonna help him one bit."

"Ahhh, shit! You think X's gonna kill 'im?"

"If that nigga had somebody take our shit, hell yeah!"

"Well, just make sure X gets my jewelry back before he pulls the plug on Neeko's grimey ass!"

"Don't worry, he will. But you're gonna need to do me a favor too."

"What's up?"

"If he ever decides to call you and acts like he wants to see you, act like you want to see him too. But before you set up something with him, call me first so I can let X know what's going on, OK?"

"OK," I said, even though I felt uneasy about it.

I knew right away that Carmen would want me to set Neeko up, and I wasn't up for that. Setting niggas up to get murdered was not cool and I didn't want any part of it. I couldn't have his blood on my hands. Now all I had to do was stay the hell away from him. He was bad news!

Carmen and I ended our conversation with her promising that she wouldn't divulge any of the information I had just discussed with her about me being in that shootout with Neeko. She vowed not to say a word, mentioning the fact that she hadn't spoken to Kira since she left the shop, so I had nothing to worry about.

"I'm closer to you than her, so why would I talk to her about your business? I mean, Kira and I are cool, but we ain't cool like you and I are."

"Yeah, a'ight," I said and then we both laughed and a planned a lunch date for the next day.

After we hung up, I couldn't help but wonder if in fact Neeko did have something to do with the robbery. If he did, he'd better watch his back because if he knew like I knew, his life was about to end. Yeah, he escaped death not too long ago and that didn't happen too often. So he'd better pay up on his insurance policy and update his will because he was definitely on his way with a one-way ticket to see his maker. And I wasn't talking about the man above either. The way this nigga carried on, I knew he had made a deal with the devil, and he was about to pay up.

Playing the Field
(Nikki Speaks)

Not too long after I got off the phone with Carmen, I called Fatu. He said he was at the club so he was kind of busy, but I got him to stay on the phone long enough to ask him about his engagement to my cousin. "I saw the ring," I didn't hesitate to say.

"She showed it to you?"

"I couldn't help but see it. It was almost bigger than her knuckle."

Fatu chuckled. "It is beautiful, huh?"

"Yeah, it's nice. But what I want to know is, are you sure you want to do this?"

"Yes, I am more than sure. I love her." His accent was stronger than ever.

"You don't really mean that! And besides, she doesn't deserve you."

"I need her in my life to balance the issues I'm currently dealing with."

"But what about me? I told you that you and I would have been good together."

"I know, I know, but I'm dealing with some major shit right now, and I believe she can help bring the good out of me."

"Trust me, she can't bring the good out of no one." I hoped my comment would open up his mind to the possibility that she might be the wrong one for him.

"Listen, Nikki, you are a beautiful woman, but this is something I must do."

It was becoming evident that this nigga wasn't trying to hear me, so I snapped and let the cat out of the bag. "Look, I can't take this shit any longer. You are about to make the biggest mistake of your life. She isn't going to make you happy! I'm the one for you. I would do anything for you. She is going to use you and then toss you aside as soon as the next man comes along."

"Calm down, Nikki,"

"Calm down for what? You're not listening to me. I'm trying to tell you some real stuff!"

"Listen, sweetie, you're getting yourself worked up for nothing. Remember we have a bond that no one can break. Now come on down to the club so we can have a drink and talk some more. Believe me, everything will be OK. I will make sure of that."

I sighed. "All right."

Saying "I Do"
(Kira Speaks)

Today was Carmen's wedding day, and since Fatu elected not to go, Nikki and I got dressed and headed over to the church. Everything was so elegant and beautiful. There had to be at least 150 guests in attendance. The church was filled with a multitude of lavender and white roses and tall, glowing candles, and the wooden pews were decorated with clusters of ivy and white bows. Carmen walked down the aisle in a pair of Jimmy Choo shoes and a platinum, fitted Yves St. Laurent bridal gown made of satin and tulle, generously dusted with Swarovski crystals. She wore her hair in an upsweep with a diamond tiara fastened to a lengthy chiffon veil. Believe me, the chick looked like a fucking princess.

Xavier stood beside the pastor, ready to greet his bride, wearing a three-piece ivory Armani suit, complete with white tails and a white top hat. You could tell he was nervous, but he managed to keep his cool.

After the two came face to face, they recited their heartfelt vows and took turns slipping on their diamond wedding bands. Moments later they lit a unity candle.

"I now pronounce you man and wife," the pastor said. "You may kiss the bride."

Xavier and Carmen embraced one another and kissed passionately. Then they paid homage to their African-American heritage by jumping the broom. The ceremony was so beautiful that Nikki and I both cried.

"I want my wedding to be just like this one," I commented.

"Yeah, it was nice, huh?"

"It sure was," I said as we watched Carmen and Xavier leave the church.

Outside, a 2008 Maybach 57 waited to escort them to their reception. They were doing it real big, if you asked me. The reception was held in the ballroom of the Grand Hyatt Hotel. The chairs, tables, and walls were draped in varying of shades of lavender and white silk fabric. Bouquets of roses in the same color scheme were held aloft by candelabra centerpieces. The entire wedding, from start to finish, was perfectly put together.

During the reception, the food was set up buffet style, and Nikki and I dug into steak, shrimp in lobster sauce, scallops wrapped in bacon, and the sautéed green beans. We also sipped on a couple glasses of Cristal. Later we enjoyed chocolate truffles by Sweeties Candy Drops before we nibbled on a piece of white, four-tiered wedding cake embellished with lavender sugar roses. The food was off the charts. The whole event was really festive and I thoroughly enjoyed myself.

Before I retired for the night, I greeted the newlyweds and wished them the best.

"Thanks so much for inviting me," I said to the happy couple.

"Thanks for coming," they both replied with wide smiles.

"So, where do y'all go from here?"

"We're gonna stay here for the night because we have a room upstairs in the Presidential Suite. But we're leaving early in the morning for Turks and Caicos," Carmen stated.

"Oh, I bet that's gonna be nice! How long are y'all staying?"

"Six nights and seven days."

"Oh my goodness! Y'all are going to have some fun!" I smiled. "Don't come back pregnant now," I teased.

"Oh, it's too late for that. We gon' start working on that tonight," Xavier interjected with a chuckle.

I smiled back. "Good luck!"

I wished them much happiness and gave them a little advice about keeping people out of their business. They took everything in and thanked me once again for coming. On my way out, I saw Nikki smiling in this guy's face, so I walked over to her and told her that I was about to leave, since she and I both rode together.

"How you doing? I'm Nikki's cousin, Kira," I said to the guy, extending my hand.

"I'm doing fine." He shook my hand. "I'm Nate."

"Nice to meet you, Nate." I turned to Nikki, who had her face all screwed up because I'd just introduced myself to her new friend. I didn't know what she thought, but I wasn't going to make moves on him, so she could've kept that expression to herself. "Are you leaving with me? Because I'm ready to go."

"Can you wait five minutes, please?" Her tone reflected her irritation.

I didn't feed into her drama. "I'll be in the car."

A few minutes later she got into the car. We didn't say a word to one another the entire drive home. This whole thing with her attitude was really getting on my fucking nerves. She acted like she really couldn't stand me. I mean, damn, was it that bad?

Immediately after we got back to the house, Nikki went her way and I went mine. I walked into the house, took off my clothes, flopped down on the sofa, turned on the TV and reminisced on how beautiful Carmen's wedding was. I could only imagine that my wedding to Fatu would be more glamorous than Carmen's. I mean, he and I both had more money than her and Xavier, so our expensive taste would be way over the top. While I was dreaming of my fairytale wedding, my cell phone rang. I didn't bother to look at the CallerID.

"Hello," I said.

"Hello, beautiful," Fatu said.

I smiled. "Hello to you too, handsome. And how was your day?"

"It was fine. How was the wedding?"

"Oh my God, Fatu, it was so beautiful. I wished you could have been there so you could get an idea of what I want our wedding to be like."

"There's no need to fret, baby. Everything is going to be all right. I've already got you scheduled to meet with a couple of wedding planners this coming week, so everything will be absolutely perfect."

"What day?"

"I'm sure it's Thursday. But, I'm gonna have to check my book to make sure."

"So, what are you doing later?"

"Why? Do you want to see me?" he asked.

"You know I do."

"Okay, well give me a couple of hours to take care of a few things around here at the club and then I'll call you so we can meet up at my place and have a quiet night alone."

"All right. Sounds like a plan," I told him and then we blew each other a kiss and hung up.

After we ended our call, I hopped up off the sofa and slipped on a pair of my running sneakers. Since I had absolutely nothing to do, I headed down to the salon so I could straighten up a few things around there. When I pulled up curbside it was a little after eight PM and I noticed Sophie and another Nigerian chick coming out of her shop.

I turned off my ignition, got out of the car, and walked straight to my front door. I tried avoiding eye contact with them, but Sophie and the other chick stood there and waited for the right opportunity to get my attention. "I met your fiancé the other day while he was leaving your salon, and I must say that he's a very nice guy."

"Thank you." I smiled.

"So, when is the big day?" she continued.

"We haven't set a date yet," I lied, hoping she'd take the hint and carry her nosey ass. Shit, we weren't cool like that for her to be asking me a whole lot of damn questions.

"Well, I hate to be the bearer of bad news, but it's not going work," she replied, placing her hand on her hip.

As hard as it was, I kept the smile on my face and said, "Well, thanks for the heads up," and then I put the key in the door to unlock it.

"You and your fucking cousin are nothing but whores. Y'all need to stay away from our men. Stay with your own kind and leave our men alone," she roared.

Listening to this ignorant-ass bitch rant and rave about me and Nikki being whores and that my marriage to Fatu wasn't going to work made my skin crawl. I honestly tried my best to avoid this bitch, but she pressed my buttons this time, so I let her ugly ass have it. "Listen, bitch, don't you have some fucking monkeys to run down behind?

"Excuse me!"

"No bitch! Excuse me," I snapped back. "You are always walking around here starting shit with me. Stop worrying about what the fuck is going on over here and worry about who your husband is sticking his little-ass dick in. And for your information, there are no whores over here. We are nothing but women with class who wouldn't tolerate a man we are fucking to have two and three wives. See, that shit only happens in Africa, not here. So, the next time you come at me with some bullshit, make sure you come correct because I ain't gonna be so nice." I opened my door and closed behind me before she could utter another word.

I did, however, look through my mini-blinds to see if she was going to walk her dusty ass on over, but she didn't. Instead, she said a few words in her native language and got the hell on in her car. I, on the other hand, took a seat in the back office and exhaled. All I could think about was those two big bitches whooping my little ass. Thank God for all that space we had between us because I believe if she'd been just a little bit closer to me, then she probably would have knocked my ass out. And I would not have been ready for that. So, from that day forward I vowed to keep my ass at least ten feet away from her. I was too old and too pretty to be getting fucked up in this day and time. And that's some real shit!

On the Prowl

(Nikki Speaks)

After Kira and I left Carmen's reception, I got dropped off at my car. I didn't say thank you or anything. I just wanted to get the hell away from her as quickly as possible. I ended up dipping up to the club to hang out with Fatu, but he wasn't there. Bintu wasn't there either, so I sat around and had a few drinks. Meanwhile, this chick comes up to the bar and asks me if she could buy me a drink. I looked at her like she was fucking crazy. I mean, what kind of pickup line was that? Did I look like I needed somebody to buy me a drink? So I said, "No, I'm fine." But this ho was persistent.

"Are you sure?" she asked.

Now don't get me wrong, she was beautiful as hell. She was very tall and lean like a model. Her hair was cut short in a tapered style, and it was really pretty because her hair was naturally curly. She was dressed in an expensive Carolina Herrera dress like she had a lot of zeros at the bottom of her bank statement. But I wasn't impressed by that bullshit. I had money too, so I let her know it.

"Yes, I'm sure. Believe me, I have a black card in my purse that'll pretty much take care of anything I need," I lied.

She smiled. "Sounds like American Express. We have something in common."

I ignored her and took another sip of my drink.

"Are you here alone?" she wanted to know.

"Yes."

"Me too. But hopefully I won't be for long."

"There are plenty of eligible men in here, so take your pick."

"I'm more of a connoisseur. I like both sexes."

I almost choked on my drink after this bitch told me she was bisexual. I honestly did not know how to respond to that. I mean, I'd always thought about the possibility of having a threesome, but I never thought I would have a chick approach me with so much aggression. She was making me nervous as hell. Thank God Fatu came over from out of nowhere.

"How's it going over here?" he asked.

"I am so glad to see you," I said quickly.

"What's going on?" he wanted to know.

"Nothing much. Just sitting here sipping on my Long Island, talking to this lady."

"Well, don't let me interrupt," he said and began to back up in the direction he had come from.

I quickly grabbed his arm, preventing him from leaving. "Let me talk to you for a minute," I insisted.

"Sure, what's up?"

"Excuse me," I said to the woman and then I stood. I pulled Fatu to the other side of the club and reiterated every word of my conversation with that chick. And then I told him how I always wanted to experience a threesome, but never had the nerve to do it. Fatu stood there with the weirdest expression on his face.

"So what are you going to do?" he finally asked.

"What do you mean?"

"Are you going to take her up on her offer?"

I laughed. "Yeah, if you join in with us."

He hesitated for a second and then said, "I'm not sure if I can handle both of y'all."

"I can't speak for her, but I'll take it easy on you."

"I can't do it tonight. Kira is coming by my place later."

"Fuck her!"

"Come on," he said, massaging my shoulders, "let's do this another night."

"When?"

"Just get her number and tell her you'll call her tomorrow."

"You sure?"

"Yes, I'm sure," he told me and then he walked off.

When I returned to the bar homegirl was still sitting there sipping on her drink. She was heavily engaged in a conversation with this other cat, so I sat back and let her do her thing. But right after he walked off, she and I chatted for a bit. After she told me her name was Crissy and that she owned a travel agency across town, I got her number and told her that I would love her to buy me that drink she had offered earlier. After I got my drink I got to know her a little more. I wasn't about to tell her anything about my life, though. She was just going to be a one-night stand and my one chance to show Fatu how much I could really be down for him.

A couple of days later Fatu and I got with Crissy at her condo and believe it or not, shit went down that night. I had never in my life been with a man and another woman at the same time, so it was an experience I'd never forget. As a matter-of-fact, I could definitely see myself partaking in one of those rendezvous again, because Fatu did his motherfucking thing maneuvering back and forth between the two of us. I got mad a few times when I saw how good he was fucking Crissy. He was digging in her ass for days and the expression he was giving was that of a man who was enjoying himself. At one point, I thought he'd forgotten about me because he wouldn't let up off that chick. He had to have been on her for at least twenty minutes straight, and I didn't like that shit at all. I told him how I felt when it was all over, so you know he apologized to me and assured me that he would never make me feel like that again. I walked away with a smile and a pocketful of gratification, so I was cool. Too bad we didn't video record the whole thing. I would've loved to show it off to Kira, because I know it would've definitely stopped the wedding then and I would have Fatu all to myself for sure.

Going into Stalking Mode

(Kira Speaks)

I'd been having some major anxiety attacks lately. They all stemmed from feelings I'd been having about Fatu. He'd been doing a lot of disappearing acts these last couple of weeks, saying he was working late at the club, but when I went by there a few times to check on him, the motherfucker wasn't there. Last night was a perfect example of how he got lost. I called his cell phone and he didn't answer it. I called his nightclub, and no one seemed to know where the fuck he was at. This lasted the entire night. I didn't get to talk to Fatu until around two AM, and when I finally talked to him, he had a whole bunch of excuses about how he fell asleep over his cousin's house. Yeah, right! That was a bullshit lie, and he knew that I knew it, but I didn't have any proof.

I had a trick for his ass on this day, though. I was geared up and ready, especially after he told me he had to run to the liquor store and get a list of shit for the club because the truck didn't deliver his shipment of alcohol that day. I slipped on my black Juicy Couture sweat suit jacket and put on my all-black Ed Hardy trucker cap. I wanted to keep a low profile while I was tailing Fatu.

I left the shop around eight-thirty PM, and I told Rachael that she'd have to lock up because I was about to go on a mission. She assured me that she'd be OK, so I hopped in my whip and left. The entire drive to nightclub, all I could think about was Fatu. I had made up my mind that I was going to sit outside his fucking nightclub all night if I had to, just to see what type of games he was playing. I needed to know who he was fucking and where she lived.

When I arrived at the club, I parked my car a block and a half away, so I could get a good view of who went in and came out. But after about two and a half hours of that bullshit, I realized that Fatu wasn't going to show up. At that moment, I started up my engine and headed over to Fatu's apartment. While I waited for him to appear, Fatu called me. I got scared because I thought he saw me waiting outside.

"Hello," I said.

"Hi, baby. Where are you?" he asked. I immediately figured that could see me.

"Why? Where am I supposed to be?" I asked, trying to see what he knew.

"You're supposed to be here fucking me," he said. I could tell he was smiling.

"I'm at the shop," I lied.

"Oh, OK. Well, I'm gonna chill in the house for the rest of the night." Just as Fatu told me that, I saw him coming out of his building. Fatu was a fucking liar!

"Fatu, I'm working on my last client, so I'll call you back," I lied again. I needed to get off the phone with him and be ready to follow his ass. Sure enough, Fatu jumped in his ride after Hakim drove it out of the valet parking lot. I waited for three cars to pass and pulled out into traffic after Fatu. He hopped on Highway 290 and headed northeast, toward Rice Village. He dipped in and out of traffic like his mind was going bad, but I hung in there with him, all the while being careful not to get spotted. Then, out of the blue, a fucking sixteen-wheeler jumped right in front of me.

"Move, bitch!" I screamed. The truck inched along, and I swear, I had to have been behind him for at least two miles. I tried to move into the next lane, but the other cars whizzed past so fast, I couldn't make a move. "Fuck!" I yelled in frustration. I knew I had lost Fatu.

When I finally made it around this big-ass rig, Fatu's car was nowhere in sight. Tears immediately welled up in my eyes. Now I was really frustrated and pissed.

"Urrrrggghhh! Where the fuck are you?" I screamed, letting the tears run down my face. I knew he was up to something, and I wanted so badly to find out where he was going and who he was going to see. I fucked up, though, and wouldn't get that chance now.

I took the next exit, which was Bernard Drive, and made a U-turn to get back on the highway. There was really nothing else for me to do but go home.

Exasperated, I slowly pulled into my driveway. I had so much shit on my mind, I couldn't even see straight. I climbed out of my car and skulked toward my front door. After I threw my keys and handbag onto the coffee table in the living room, I flopped down on the sofa and wondered where the hell Fatu could've gone. I picked up my cordless phone and dialed his number. The motherfucker didn't answer. It rang once and went directly to voice mail.

"Son of a bitch!" I screamed and threw the cordless phone against the wall.

Later that night my telephone rang while I was knocked out. I didn't bother to look at the CallerID because my eyes weren't focused enough to see the numbers anyway.

"Hello," I said, sounding out of it.

"Kira, wake up! This is Carmen."

"Who?" I asked, wanting the caller to repeat herself.

"It's me, Carmen."

I yawned and looked around at my alarm clock. It read one-thirty AM, so I immediately knew something was wrong because Carmen never called my house this late, not even when she worked for me at the shop.

"What's the matter?" I asked.

"I just got a call from Nikki and she was crying, talking about she had gotten herself in a lot of shit and she was not going to be able to undo what she'd done, but she wouldn't say what it was. So I was thinking that maybe if you called her she would talk to you."

"Carmen, I hate to be the bearer of bad news, but Nikki and I aren't on it like that. She stays out of my business and I do the same. So whatever she's got going on, I'm sure she'll figure out a way to get out of it. She's a big girl. She'll be all right," I assured her.

Carmen seemed offended. "Damn! It's like that? I see why she doesn't fuck with you anymore," she commented.

"Good! Now that makes two of us," I said, and then I pressed down on the end button and put the phone back on the base.

I lay back in my bed and thought about what it was that Nikki was trying to tell Carmen. I figured it probably had something to do with a man, so I immediately dismissed the thought and buried my head in my pillow. But then it hit me that I still hadn't spoken with Fatu, so I slid back across my bed and reached for the cordless phone. I had this nigga on speed dial, so I pressed the appropriate number. His phone rang one time and then went straight to voice mail. My blood pressure went sky high.

"What the fuck is going on with this nigga?" I wondered aloud.

It took everything within me not to slip on a pair of sweats and some sneakers and go look for this nigga. I was known for stalking out a nigga's spot if I suspected him of fucking around on me. I mean, it wasn't nothing for me to sit outside a guy's house for hours on end, especially if my intuition was killing me. But since there was no guarantee that he was even at home, I figured it was best that I chill on out before I went out there and ran into somebody else's whip out of mere frustration.

I could, however, call the club to see if the motherfucker was there. Bintu answered the phone, and I didn't hesitate to ask him where Fatu was.

"He's not here," he said, his accent really strong.

"Then where is he?" I snapped.

"I'm not sure. I haven't seen him for a few hours now."

"Are you expecting him to come back?"

"Well, a couple hours ago he said he was running out and that he'd be back, but he hasn't shown up yet and the club is about to close."

"OK, well when he gets back tell him I am really pissed off with him and that he better have a good damn excuse of why his phone is going straight to voice mail."

"All right. I will relay the message."

"Thanks," I said and ended the call.

Once again I had hit a brick wall. This nigga was still out there in them motherfucking streets. And the fucked-up thing about it was that I didn't know where. Bintu didn't even know where he was, and that was mind boggling. But it would be all right, because as soon as I got my hands on this nigga, I was going to kill him. I was not going to go through this same shit all over again. I had put up with enough shit from Ricky and his bitches! I would be damned if I went through that mess again. He'd die first.

Your Heart Don't Lie

(Kira Speaks)

When Fatu finally called, which was the next morning, he told me he wanted to take me out to lunch. I took him up on his offer because I wanted to meet him face to face when I put his ass on the hot seat. While I sat across from Fatu in Ruth's Chris, picking at my food, I made little innuendos about him fucking around on me, but he played it off very well. As a matter-of-fact, he acted like he was hard of hearing. I knew better, though, and he knew I knew it too.

See, things had definitely changed between us. A lot of his time was unaccounted for lately. Fatu was always telling me he had this or that to take care of, but it was never anything I could verify. With Bintu and all the other guys running the nightclub, he didn't have to be there as much, so when I was in the shop late at night, working miracles on my clients' heads, he had a lot of idle time. A few times the nigga did a couple of disappearing acts. When the shit started happening, it took me back to my days with Ricky. It wasn't something I took lightly. My instincts told me there was someone else.

I finally looked up from my plate and glanced at Fatu. He was distracted. The pretty Hispanic waitress had stopped to check on us, and as she pranced away from our table I watched Fatu follow her with his eyes. *Would you look at this motherfucker? Does he really think I'm stupid?* I wondered, rolling my eyes in disgust.

At first our relationship had been what some might consider a whirlwind love affair. We use to do everything together and he didn't spare any expenses, especially when he flew me first class to Cancun for four days. That weekend was so fucking nice. This nigga had us equipped with concierge services and the whole nine. In addition to that, this cat would send me roses on the regular and he'd even cook for me. Now how many cats you know send their girls flowers and cook for them on a regular? Not too many. That's why I held on to his ass. And what's really weird is that after only three months of dating, we were engaged. My head told me to be careful, but my heart told me to give it a try. Now I stared across the table at Fatu and wanted to slap the shit out of him.

"What did you say happened to your hand and neck again?" I asked, referring to the deep scratches Fatu had on his hand, and the welts on his neck.

"Kira, didn't I just tell you that I got into a scuffle with some drunk guy before I left the club last night while me and one of the bouncers were throwing him out?" he asked dismissively, shoveling a forkful of steak into his mouth.

I looked down at my drink, contemplating whether to throw the shit in his face. What it looked like to me was that he and his bitch must've had rough sex, and she scratched his ass up.

"Yeah, you told me, but those scratches look like they came from a chick's nails," I replied, twisting my lips into a snarl. Fatu didn't know I'd searched his shit at home and found lipstick on one of his dress shirts a few weeks ago. I didn't say anything at the time, because all he would've done was blame it on a female customer he hugged at the club. I figured I'd gather a little more evidence before I confronted him.

"Look, Kira, I told you where they came from. You should be happy just to be with me. I told you many times that I could have any woman I want," Fatu replied. He always remained calm, even when he was being accused. That shit pissed me off even more. What really got under my skin was when he reminded me that as a wealthy, single, heterosexual man he could have any woman he wanted.

"I know what you told me, but my intuition tells me that your ass may be cheating," I shot back, throwing my napkin onto the table.

Fatu remained silent. I folded my arms across my chest and gave him the silent treatment right back. Neither of us looked at each other. He pushed food around on his plate and I occasionally played with the straw in my drink. Anger welled up inside me and I finally exploded.

"You know what? You can sit there and play dumb all you want," I said in a low, angry whisper, "but I know what time it is. If you think I'm going to sit around while you go out and collect scratches from other bitches, then you're sadly mistaken!" I felt like I was going to burst into tears.

"Relax, Kira. I love only you." Fatu took my hand into his, trying to hide his scratches, and then kissed me. I smiled inside when he said he loved me, but I kept a straight face. I wanted to believe that he wouldn't cheat. I'd taken enough shit from Ricky and Russ. I wasn't trying to go down that same road again.

After our disagreement, Fatu and I didn't speak to each other during the entire drive home. I made up my mind that I was going to stop acting paranoid and just let him love me, because whether or not I believed it, I was about to be married all over again. This time around, I was going to be happy and rich, and maybe be a mother too.

"Are you going home with me?" Fatu asked.

"If you want me to," I answered.

"What kind of answer is that? You know I love it when you're with me. Why you think I keep bugging you about moving in with me?" He reached for my hand.

"Let's not get into that again. I told you to wait until after the wedding."

"I know, I know. But can you blame me? Look at you! You're beautiful! So when I can't share my bed with you every night, it bothers me."

I smiled because everything he said sounded heartfelt. I reminded him that our wedding date was less than a month away, so we didn't have long at all to be together. He bought that line tonight, but I knew that in a couple of days I would be hearing him whine about our living arrangements again.

Fatu used a digital cardkey to open the huge French doors at the entrance of his apartment. I always felt like royalty when I came over. Walking inside, the smell of jasmine was in the air. I could tell the housekeeper had made a house call today because there wasn't a dust ball in sight. I took off my shoes and flopped down on the love seat. Fatu walked upstairs. I flicked on his sixty-five-inch HDTV that hung over his fireplace and began channel surfing. I ended up at the eleven o'clock news. I wasn't really into the news, and I was about to change the channel when a story caught my attention. I listened intently as the reporter spoke.

"Police say that a fifth woman was found murdered in her home on Jones Road, near Highway 290. Police Chief Ray Biggs would not confirm the manner of death of this last victim, but the chief did say that the victim put up a fierce struggle and may have injured her assailant. Police believe that all five murders are related. All of the women were murdered in their homes, and all lived in upscale neighborhoods. Police are asking all women to watch their surroundings as they go home, and to make a note if they see anyone suspicious following them or lurking around."

The news report spooked me out. I couldn't believe that there might be a serial killer in my neighborhood.

"What is that you are watching?" Fatu's voice boomed behind me. I jumped and dropped the remote.

"Don't sneak up on me like that! You scared the shit out of me," I gasped, holding my chest.

"What are you afraid of?" He chuckled.

"There's a serial killer in the area, killing women. They said that they believe the guy is following the women home, and then killing them in their houses. That is something I need to be aware of."

"Oh, I'm sure that once he kidnaps you, with all of that mouth you got, he would set you free quickly," Fatu joked as he sat next to me.

"That's not funny." I rolled my eyes and inched away from him, because I knew what he wanted. I got up and said, "I'm going to take a shower." I lied.

"I'll be here waiting." He smiled and touched his dick.

I rushed upstairs. Although I said I wasn't going to think about Fatu with other women anymore, or about him cheating, I couldn't help it. I knew I had a few minutes to search through his shit before he came upstairs to join me in the shower. I crept into his bedroom. Everything was in its place. Fatu kept his shit so neat, I swore he was obsessive-compulsive.

"Shit," I whispered. I didn't have much time. I decided to go to the walk-in closet first. If I got busted in there it wouldn't seem so bad, since I had a small section of the closet for my own clothes. Looking around the closet, I could tell Fatu had been inside. His dirty clothes bin had one shirt sticking out. I frowned. That was unlike him.

I walked over to the bin and lifted the top. I wanted to sniff the boxers he last wore to see if I smelled any pussy juice or saw any cum stains, because if I did, then it was going to be on. As I dug into the bin and searched for the boxers, my hands landed on a white tee. The shirt had a little bit of blood smeared across the bottom of it, and I could tell that if he put on the shirt, the blood spot would hang right above his groin area.

"What the fuck is this?" I asked aloud.

"Kira!" Fatu called. My heart almost jumped out of my chest. I hurriedly stuffed everything back into the hamper. I whirled around, trying to make sure everything was the way he left it.

"Kira?" Fatu called out again, walking into the closet.

I tried to hide my agitation. "Yes? What is it?"

"What are you doing?"

"I'm trying to get something to change into before I hop into the shower," I said nervously, faking like I was eager to fuck him. Fatu looked at me strangely, then he looked around the closet. He looked back at me with a suspicious glare. I smiled a crooked, nervous smile.

"Need some help?"

"Nah, I'm cool. I got it. Now go and get in the bed."

"All right. But hurry up and shower. My dick is getting impatient." He walked out of the closet.

I felt like throwing up and my hands shook as I went into the bathroom. I couldn't help but think about the bloodied T-shirt in Fatu's closet. The only thing that surfaced in my mind was that he fucked some nasty-ass ho while she was on her fucking period. How fucking disgusting could he be? What was he doing, trying to get AIDS or something? Whatever it was he was out there doing, it didn't sit well with me at all, so something was going to have to give.

As I was about to head into the shower, I immediately thought back to a sexual episode between me and Fatu that had freaked me out.

One night while making love, Fatu was going crazy, like he loved the pussy. All of a sudden he flipped me over, pulled me up on my hands and knees, and forcefully rammed his dick into my asshole. I was not ready for his brutality, and I screamed in pain and grabbed handfuls of the Egyptian cotton sheets. Fatu ignored my screams, grabbed me around the neck, and pulled me closer to him. He rammed me in the ass like an animal while I cried and screamed. Then, just as quickly as he started, he stopped. He growled like an animal as he came. I collapsed on the bed and curled into a fetal position, crying in pain. Fatu finally realized that I was in severe pain, and he rolled over to comfort me.

He told me that he didn't mean to hurt me, but that my sex was so good he'd gotten carried away. I was so in love with Fatu at the time, I just accepted his explanation. That night he held me and caressed me like no man had done since Ricky. I wanted to be loved so badly that I overlooked all of Fatu's sexual hang-ups. I figured that one day I would get used to it. But now I wondered. I knew I couldn't get used to him cheating.

By the time I came out of the bathroom, Fatu had fallen asleep. I was relieved. I stood in the doorway of the bedroom and watched him for a minute, then I noticed the light flashing on his iPhone. He had a text message.

Who the fuck is texting him this time of night? I wondered. *It must be his bitch!*

I tiptoed over to the dresser, picked up the phone, and quickly pressed the button to read his text.

WE GOT A PRIVATE PARTY GOING ON IN THE VIP ROOM! PUT KIRA TO BED & COME JOIN US!

The message was from Bintu. I automatically assumed that they had some strippers up at the club, shaking their stinking asses for a few dollars. I didn't know what Bintu had going on in his fucking mind, but Fatu wasn't about to go nowhere. I wanted to let Bintu know this personally, but I used Fatu's phone to call him back.

"What's up, brother?" Bintu answered.

"Nah, it's me, Kira," I replied with an attitude.

"Oh . . . um, hey, Kira." He stumbled over his greeting.

"Hey to you too, Bintu."

"Um . . . where is Fatu?"

"He's asleep, since he didn't have to put me to bed. So he won't be able to join you at your party in the VIP room."

Bintu was silent for a moment. He knew he'd been busted. "All right. Well when he wakes up in the morning, let him know that I was trying to get in touch with him."

"All right."

Right after I hung up with Bintu, I pressed the Menu key on Fatu's phone and scrolled through his call history. To my surprise, his entire incoming and missed call lists were filled with the number 713-555-7979, which was Nikki's fucking number.

Why the hell is her number in his phone so many times? I mean, what part of the game is this? What the hell is really going on? I wondered.

Shit, was I going to have to call her ass up so I could get to the bottom of this thing? Or should I step to this clown and ask him? I mean, two stories were better than one because I knew they were both going to come up with some bogus ass shit. I decided to call Nikki's ass first.

While I was dialing and waiting for her phone to ring my heart started beating uncontrollably, but it stopped the second Nikki said hello.

"Nikki, what's going on between you and Fatu?" I didn't hesitate to ask.

Nikki hesitated and then she said, "Who the fuck is this?"

"Cut it out, drama queen! You know who it is!" I spat back.

"Why the fuck are you calling me?"

"No . . . no . . . no . . . sweetie, I'm the one asking questions. So explain to me why the hell you are calling my fiancé so damn much."

"Because I be doing little odd jobs at the club for him, that's why."

"Come on now, Nikki, when did you start working at the club?"

Irritated by my question, she said, "About a few weeks now, right after I left the shop."

"Well, what do you do for him?"

"Look, I ain't got time for all this shit! Ask him!" she roared and then she ended the call.

I was still feeling uneasy about the whole thing, because now I was wondering why Fatu never told me that Nikki was working at the club. I mean, it wasn't a big deal, but I would have expected him to mention it at least once in an indirect way. Then again, maybe he figured that I wouldn't want to know. Whatever his reason, it would all come out sooner or later. I knew Nikki would tell him that I called her, but I could care less.

After I set Fatu's iPhone back down, I quietly slid into bed next to him. I really wanted to go home, but it was too late, so I would spend the night next to a man I was starting to believe was a complete stranger.

On the Chopping Block
(Kira Speaks)

When I got up the next morning, Fatu was still asleep. I left him in bed and got dressed to go home. Before I walked out, I left him a note on the refrigerator, telling him I had to run off because I had an appointment to see my dressmaker. The lie sounded good, so I knew he'd believe it. Upon my arrival at home, Nikki was busy in the kitchen cooking some French toast, which was shocking to see because she didn't do too much cooking. As I walked farther into the kitchen, I noticed that she wasn't just cooking for herself. Suddenly her attitude last night made sense.

The stranger saw me first. "Hey, what's up?" he greeted.

"Good morning," I replied to the strange man, trying to be polite. In all actuality, I was pissed. We had rules in this house, and one of them was that men weren't allowed to come to the house until after we'd known them for at least three months. I'd never seen this cat before in my life, so I knew Nikki's silly ass had just met him. Not only that, this nigga was sitting around my house in his fucking boxers, like he lived there, so I knew she fucked him last night.

Why would she let a nigga she'd just met come and fuck her where she laid her head? How stupid and desperate could she be? What, he couldn't take her to his place, or to a hotel? See, that's what's wrong with females today. We're always making shit easy for these niggas. Let their asses get out here and go the extra mile for us, not the other way around. I sighed deeply. There was no use in me getting all upset, because she wasn't ever going to learn.

Nikki placed two slices of French toast on the guy's plate and then she looked up and saw me. "Whatcha doing home so early?" she asked as she fidgeted slightly with embarrassment.

"I've got some errands to run, but I wanted to come home and change into something more comfortable." I bit down on my bottom lip to keep from saying anything I would regret, especially in front of a stranger.

"What time are you leaving?" she asked as if she was trying to rush me out of there.

"I'm not sure. Maybe in another hour or so." I looked at the stranger again. "So, who is your new friend?"

"This is Nate. He's Carmen's husband's homeboy."

"Oh, yeah, I remember seeing you at the wedding. You were the best man."

Nate smiled, revealing his white set of teeth. He wasn't all that handsome, but he had nice, smooth skin, a freshly cut Caesar with long side burns, and his body was nice, so I guess he was doable. I was sure that Nikki's hot ass felt the same way.

"So how long y'all been talking?" I pressed.

"Since the wedding." Nikki's reply had a hint of a brag to it as she took a seat next to Nate.

"Oh, so y'all been seeing each other for about a month now, huh?"

Nikki smiled. "Yep."

I turned my attention back to Nate. "So, Nate, tell me, what do you do for a living?"

"I'm into buying and selling real estate."

"Oh really? That's nice. But tell me, how are you buying and selling houses when the housing market is still so bad?" I knew his ass was lying. The real estate market was really fucked up, and hardly anyone was buying houses, especially since a lot of banks weren't lending money like they used to.

"Why are you being so nosey? Let the man eat in peace!" Nikki interjected.

"Do you think I'm being nosey?" I asked Nate, but Nikki wasn't backing down. She did not want me questioning this nigga for nothing in the world.

"You a'ight," Nate forced himself to say.

I sensed that he was feeling a little awkward, so I left his dumb ass alone and got a bottle of apple juice from the refrigerator. Just as I was about to pour myself a glass, my phone rang. I checked the CallerID. It was Fatu. I contemplated not answering, but since I knew I wasn't going to be in the mood to explain later why I didn't answer, I went ahead and answered.

"Hello," I said, almost whispering.

"Kira, why did you leave without waking me!" Fatu screamed into the phone.

"Fatu, I had to come home. I left you a note," I explained.

"What time are you going to be done?"

"I'm not sure. Why?"

"Because I wanted to take you to a spa today."

"Well, I'm just gonna have to call you when I'm done with my plans."

"OK. I'll probably be at the club, taking care of a few things."

"All right," I said and hung up.

I noticed Nikki gritting on me, so I put away my Blackberry. "What is that look for?" I asked.

"Girl, please! Stop being paranoid! Ain't nobody paying your ass no mind!" she snapped.

As badly as I wanted to blast this whore for trying to show off in front of her new boyfriend, I remained calm, poured myself a glass of juice, and said, "Yeah. All right." I walked out of the kitchen and into my bedroom. While I sat on my bed and thought about all the drama I was going through with Fatu, I overheard Nikki talking about me to that nigga Nate.

"You see she carried her ass, right?" she asked.

Nate laughed. "Yeah, I saw it."

"And you know why she did it, right?"

"Nah."

"That's because she don't fuck with me."

"Who's the oldest?"

"She is. And I used to let her run all over top of me and tell me what to do, but I shut that shit down. I told her that I was sick of it, and I wasn't taking her mess anymore."

"How long y'all been living together?"

"Since we left Virginia."

"So whose spot is this? Hers or yours?"

"Well, it's the both of ours. We went to the closing together."

I rushed back into the kitchen, filled with rage. "Yeah, we sure did. But Nicole Simpson wasn't on none of those documents I had to sign to get the keys to this place, so why don't you stop your bullshit lies!" I roared.

Nikki was shocked to see me storm back into the kitchen the way I did. Her eyes looked like they were about to pop out of her head, but since she was in the company of Nate, she wasn't going to allow me to keep embarrassing her. She came back quick on me and said, "So the fuck what, I ain't on the deed! I live here and I help you pay these bills, so don't be running up on me like you run shit!"

"You know what, Nikki? I am so sick of your mouth!" I snapped.

Nikki stood from her chair. "Do something about it!" she dared me.

"Bitch, on some real shit, you ain't worth it, so I'm going to let you slide this time. But don't you ever disrespect me in my own house again. You understand?"

"Who the fuck you think you're talking to? You ain't got no kids up in here!"

"Well, if you don't like what I'm saying, carry your ass!"

"You ain't said shit, Kira! I ain't got to be here."

"What's the holdup, then?"

"I can get out," Nikki protested.

"I don't see you moving," I told her.

"You know what, Kira? You're a funny-ass bitch! I see what you're doing."

"And what is that?"

Nikki took a couple steps toward me. "You're so jealous of me, it's a shame."

I burst into laughter. "You've got to be kidding me. Me, jealous of you?"

"Don't stand here and try to front. You know damn well you can't stand to see me doing better than you. I know you're putting me out because you want to see me fall on my face. But let me tell you something, sweetie, it ain't gonna happen, because I've got as much money as you do. So I'm going to be fine."

"That's beautiful. So when are you leaving?"

"I can get my shit out of here today," Nikki responded sarcastically.

"Make it happen then," I encouraged her.

"Come on, Nate! Help me get my shit out of here," Nikki ordered. She and Nate walked out of the kitchen.

I stood there and watched her walk into her bedroom with her company and slam the door shut. I shook my head in disgust because that bitch had a nerve to slam a door in my fucking house. I mean, who the hell did she think she was? And how dare she tell me that she had just as much money as I did? Was she on crack or something? Nikki just didn't know I had a landmine of dough piled up in my bank account, so she needed to sit her stupid ass down before I showed her something she wouldn't be able to handle.

And as far as Nikki's fuck partner back there, I sure hoped that Nate was letting her silly ass move in with him, because her ass was getting out of here once and for all. I wasn't going change my mind, either. I was so tired of that bitch's attitude, it had gotten unbearable. What got me was the fact that she walked around like somebody owed her something. That really got under my damn skin. I had a trick for her ass, though, and she definitely had it coming to her.

While I was in my bedroom changing clothes, I heard Nikki making a lot of noise in her room. It sounded like she was banging shit around in there on purpose, so that I could say something to her. I refused to feed into her shenanigans. I decided to stay my ass in the house to see if she tried to pull a stunt and fuck up some of my shit. My mother always told me that when you put a nigga out of your crib, never leave the house while they were packing, because if you did, nine times out of ten they would vandalize your house or steal some of your shit. I was going to chill right here so I could see what the hell was going on.

Nikki finally got all her shit out of my house, except for her bedroom set. She told me she'd have somebody come by with a truck to get it tomorrow, and I agreed to that. As far as her other things, it only took her about four trips between my house and her new destination to get those things out of here. I didn't know where she took her stuff, but I didn't care because it felt really good to have her ass out of my house. The way things ended, it would not surprise me if she went out and opened up her own spot like she had been planning to do all along. I honestly thought that would be the best thing she could do, because I'd had it with her drama.

But if she had it in her mind that she was going to open up a salon that would bring in more business than mine, then she had another thought coming. Her competitive ass would never build up the clientele that I had because she could not do hair. She was merely a wash girl around my salon, and she kept the books for me since she took a couple of business classes in college and was good with numbers. Aside from that, she couldn't do shit. If she thought that she was going to be successful like me, I had something special for her silly ass. Nikki would see that she was nothing like me. My clients loved me because I provided a good service, which was something she lacked, and I kept it real with them. All I could do was wish her dumb ass the best.

Rolling Solo
(Nikki Speaks)

Kira thought she did something by putting me out, but she just didn't know that she did me a favor. I was going to show that bitch that I didn't need her. For starters, I was going to fuck up her life just like she did mine. See, I was all right before I started hanging with Kira. I was attending Norfolk State University back in my hometown, and I had 3.7 GPA too. Life was pretty simple and I wasn't into any drama.

Then I get hooked up with Kira, and my life started falling apart. First I started working for her late husband Ricky, transporting his damn drugs. I admit that the money was good, but then I started fucking around with this guy named Brian, who used to work for Ricky, and that fell apart right after the narcotics agents arrested me on drug charges. From there my life got turned upside down and my parents became furious with me.

My mom and dad told me from the beginning that it wouldn't be wise for me to affiliate myself with Kira. They knew all about the dangerous but glamorous lifestyle she was living. That didn't matter to me, though, because she was family and I looked up to her. I admired everything about her. She had everything I wanted and more, so I wanted nothing else but to be in her company. I'd always been told that if you were around a person long enough, you became just like them, which was exactly what had happened to me.

Now I was a permanent fixture in her world. But instead of trying to be more and more like Kira, I was always trying to find ways to be better than her. It seemed like she and I were always in competition with one another, and it had become nerve-wracking. That was about to end, though, because I was about to get my life back on the right track. By me moving out of her place and embarking on a life of my own, everything was going to fall into place for me. I was happy as hell about it too.

Right now, though, I decided to chill at Nate's place. He told me I could bunk at his house with him until I could find an apartment. As far as my bedroom set, I planned to pick that up from Kira's house tomorrow and put it in storage.

After Nate and I finally settled down in his plush, two-bedroom townhouse, we sat around in his living room and talked for a bit. "This is really a nice place," I said to him.

He smiled at me. "Thanks."

"You know, I really appreciate you letting me stay here until I find a place."

"That's no problem."

"So, how long you been living here?" I took another look around the living room area. I admired the flat-screen TV mounted on the wall, the window treatments, not to mention the cream-colored leather sofa. Homeboy really had it hooked up in there. It wasn't fixed up in a girly type of way, but it was really nice and you could definitely tell that it belonged to a bachelor.

"Five months."

"So what's up with the other bedroom?"

"What do you mean?"

"Why is it empty?"

"Because I haven't decided if I'm going to make it a guest room. I mean, it ain't like I get a lot of company, but the few cats who do come by here to holler at me crash down here in the living room if they're too fucked up to drive home, so I might just leave it the way it is."

"Why don't you get a roommate?"

Nate shook his head. "Oh, nah, I ain't into that. Shit, I like living by myself."

"I know what you mean. It is chaotic when two people live together. So take my advice and don't rent out that room. Because if you do, you won't ever have peace of mind."

"Trust me, shorty, you ain't ever got to worry about that," he assured me and then changed the subject.

Before long he had told me more shit than he had on our first date. I can't tell you why he was holding back on me, but I am glad he finally came clean with me. He even gave me a brief history on the type of women he used to deal with. What really shocked me was when he told me that he'd just gotten out of a five-year relationship with a chick he was about to marry. Of course, I wanted to know what happened that led to the breakup. He told me that he found out she had been pregnant and had gotten an abortion behind his back. The way he said that really showed me how hurt he was behind it.

I rubbed his knee and said, "I'm sorry to hear that."

"Oh, it's all right. I'm cool."

"So, where is your ex now?"

"I don't know. But she's probably up to her same ol' tricks with the next nigga."

"Have you seen her since y'all broke up?"

"Nope. And I'm glad too."

"So how long has it been since y'all broke up?"

"Five months. Right after I moved out the crib she and I had, I got this joint."

"Oh, OK."

It finally registered with me why he wanted to live alone. But then I wondered why he was so eager to let me stay with him, especially when he'd just gotten out of a relationship. I did know one thing at least. He couldn't possibly be serious with another chick, because if he was, then he would not have asked me to come stay with him until I found a spot of my own. Knowing that I was probably the only chick in his life right then made me feel kind of special, and it gave me high hopes that maybe Nate and I could take this thing to another level. Shit, if everything worked out between us, there was a possibility that he might not want me to leave. I mean, I'd already proven to him that my pussy was good and that I liked to cook. I figured that all that was left for me to do was to keep playing the wifey role, and everything would fall into place.

This Is Not a Game
(Kira Speaks)

Fatu and I had not spoken all day. I figured he must've been taking care of business, so I didn't think to bother him until I realized that it was nine o'clock at night. Furious because I had been having some more uneasy feelings about him lately, I called him. "Where are you?" I asked without saying hello.

"I'm home."

"What have you been doing all day?"

"Taking care of business for the club."

"What are you doing at home then?"

"I wanted to change clothes."

"What time are you going back to work?"

"I'm not going back to work tonight."

"Well, where are you going?"

"I was going to surprise you and take you out, but I'm going to have to make a quick run first."

"To where?" Fatu hesitated. "Fatu, where are you going?" I asked again.

"I got to make a run by my cousin's house to pick up some money."

I knew his ass was lying. He was going to see his bitch! Whether or not he knew it, I was going too. I played it off and acted like I was fine with him making the run to his cousin's, and to add icing on the cake, I told him I loved him and that I'd be waiting. As soon as I hung up the phone, I grabbed my car keys and hauled ass to his apartment. The interstate was only three miles from my house, so I was on it in a matter of ninety seconds flat.

"Move the fuck out of the way!" I screamed at cars in front of me. My nerves unraveled as I dipped in and out of traffic. What bothered me the most was how fast my heart was beating. It felt like it was about to burst out of my damn chest, but somehow I managed to focus on my driving.

About thirty minutes later I pulled up on the side of Fatu's building's parking lot. Since it had only been thirty minutes since I'd spoken to him, I figured he might not have left yet. I waited. After about ten minutes I saw Hakim, one of the valet guys, pull Fatu's car around to the front of the building.

"Yes!" I said aloud. I hadn't missed him at all. "A'ight, Kira, make sure you don't get busted," I mumbled, giving myself a pep talk. I needed to get my mind right. First, I had to be ready for whatever I was going to see, and second, I had to be ready to drive like a maniac to keep up with Fatu.

When he finally came out of the building, I immediately looked at his attire. He was dressed in a regular black button-down shirt and a pair of black pants, and he didn't look like he was about to go out on the town. As I watched him slide into his car, I readied myself to go on the most turbulent ride of my life. I felt like Danica Patrick, getting ready for the race of my life. Soon we were off. I allowed two cars to drive in front of me as I followed Fatu, but when we got onto Highway 10, I knew I had to pick up the pace. A couple of times I let him move ahead of me about a half mile, but that was only because I vowed that I wasn't going to lose him.

Twenty minutes later he got off the Louisiana Street exit and took it all the way down to a section in Houston called Westminster Estates. I had never been to this part of Houston before, but it was very upscale. Fatu drove into the posh community and I pulled alongside a curb and waited for a few minutes. I finally got up the nerve to drive into the community so I could see whom this bitch was that he was creeping with.

About ten yards into the complex, I noticed that I was the only moving vehicle on the streets. Fatu's Bentley was nowhere in sight. I made a right turn onto the next block, which happened to be Potluck Drive, and noticed his car parked on the right side of the street, just a few yards away from another car.

"Cousin, my ass!" I said. My blood was boiling. I'd known he was lying, especially when he hesitated on the phone earlier. Not only that, I knew where all his cousins lived, and none of them were in this part of town. When we got off the Louisiana Street exit, I knew that Fatu had another agenda, and now I was about to find out who she was.

I saw movement in Fatu's car, but I couldn't see exactly what he was doing. I turned off my headlights and turned into a nearby empty driveway. All the lights were out at the house, so I pulled up to the garage door, turned off my engine, and sat there for a second as if I lived there. I didn't want to sit there too long because I knew if I did, I would draw attention to myself, so I looked over my shoulder to see what Fatu was doing, and when I saw that he was still sitting in his car, I stepped out of my car and acted as if I was about to go into the house. Thank God the front porch was built farther back from the garage, which meant that he wouldn't be able to see me walk up to the front door. When I got out of sight, I stood behind the wall, panting like I had run the fifty-yard dash. I prayed that the owners of this home wouldn't pull up anytime soon.

I listened to the crickets make their mating calls. Other than that, the neighborhood was quiet. It was somewhat spooky, which made me immediately think about that serial killer I heard about on the news. I got an uneasy feeling because I really didn't like being in the position I was in. Fatu wasn't aware that I was out there with him, so if someone decided to sneak up behind me and snatch me up, then I was going to be fucked up.

I peeped around the corner of the house and saw Fatu standing outside his car, next to the driver's side door, looking in the direction of a gray, stone-front house on the opposite side of the street. That must be where the chick lived! My heart raced like a horse. Before I could blink, this nigga walked across the street and across the lawn of the house, then disappeared down a walkway on the side of the house.

"Check out this sneaky-ass nigga!" I whispered. As badly as I wanted to walk up on his ass and bust him, I convinced myself that it would be better if I gave him enough rope to hang himself. Niggas always found a way to get out of shit when you hadn't actually caught them in the act. I wasn't going to ruin it. I needed hardcore evidence, and there was no doubt in my mind that I was going to get it that night.

"That no good motherfucker!" I growled. "And if he thinks that there's going to be a wedding after this bullshit, he's got another thing coming. Playing me like I'm some fucking joke! I mean, who the fuck does he think he is? But it's all good. He's going to definitely get what he's got coming to his ass!"

My blood pressure rose and I continued to rant to myself. As angry as I was, I started to rush up to the house and bang on the fucking door, but I held myself back. This neighborhood looked like it didn't take too kindly to ghetto chicks such as myself. Besides, I couldn't afford to get arrested for beating that bitch down. I went with plan B instead—to get that nigga on the phone and see how he would act around her.

I fumbled with my cell phone and dialed Fatu's number, but that motherfucker's voice mail picked up on the first ring. "Wait one fucking minute! Now I know this nigga ain't got his damn phone off. What kind of game is he playing? OK, now it's on and popping!" I said before I stormed back to my car.

Before I drove away from Potluck Drive, I rode right by Fatu's car and snapped two pictures of it with my Blackberry. I got a picture of his license plates, and then I took a picture of his car at an angle where that bitch's house was in full view. I couldn't see her house clearly because of how dark it was, but I could make out the distinctive stone pattern on the front of her home. I drove down the block and turned back around so I could leave out the way I came in.

When I rode back by her house, I noticed that she had turned on her bedroom light and then she suddenly walked right by her window. My heart stopped and so did my car. From the little bit I saw of her, I could tell that she was light-skinned with big titties and a head full of weave. That wasn't enough, though. I needed to get a better look at that ho. It was every woman's wish to see what the next woman looked like. It was a form of closure for us.

As I waited for her to come back past the window, the lights suddenly went off. I instantly had a meltdown and wanted to go to war. I clenched my fists and bit my bottom lip until I drew blood, but then I realized that running up in her house to whip their asses wasn't worth it. However, I did feel the need to call Fatu's phone again and leave him a nasty-ass message.

"You think you're so fucking slick, Fatu!" I yelled into my phone. "But I peeped your game out, nigga. You 'round here lying to me, telling me that you had to make a run over to your cousin's house. Nigga, you ain't went nowhere but to your bitch's house. And I got proof, so don't call me back with no lies, because it ain't gon' work this time. So do yourself a favor and stay with her, because I'm done with you. The wedding is off!" My voice screeched and then I hung up my phone. There was nothing left for me to do but carry my ass home.

No Hard Feelings
(Kira Speaks)

When I got home, I immediately poured myself a shot of Patrón. I couldn't bear the thought of Fatu fucking that bitch, or any other woman for that matter. I had literally gotten sick to my stomach and found myself walking back down the same road I went down a few times with Ricky. I remembered having these exact same feelings in the pit of my stomach. The feelings got so unbearable that I ended up pouring myself five more shots before the night was over, and then I crashed downstairs on my living room sofa.

Riiing! Riiing! Riing! The telephone jerked me out of my coma-like sleep. I grabbed it and looked at the CallerID. It was Fatu. I ignored his call. I looked at the clock and realized I had slept past the time to open up the shop, but since Rachael had a key, I figured she'd be all right. I had to know if Nikki had brought her ass into work, so I called Rachael's cell phone number. She answered on the second ring.

"Hello?"

"Hey, girl, this is Kira."

"What's up, girl? Where you at? I've been trying to call you. You got two clients in here waiting on you."

"I'm still at home. My ass had a rough night and I overslept."

"Well, what time are you coming in?"

"I'm really not in any shape to come in, Rachael. I've got a slight hangover."

"Well, what do you want me to tell your clients?"

"Tell 'em I'm sick and if they'd like, they can reschedule their appointments for tomorrow, or if you don't mind, you could do them if you're not booked up."

"Well, I only have two people in here myself, so it wouldn't be a problem. But I'll let them know what you said."

"Thanks, Rachael."

"You're welcome, girl."

"Oh, yeah, Rachael, did Nikki come into the shop yet?"

"Nope, and she hasn't called either."

"All right. Well if she does come in or call, call me and let me know."

"OK, I will. But is everything all right?"

"She and I got into it again yesterday, so I got tired of her mouth and told her it was time for her to get her ass out of my house."

"What did she say?"

"You know Nikki, Rachael. You know she tried to get all cute, especially since she had company. But I chumped her ass down and told her I wasn't trying to hear it."

"So, do you know where she is?"

"Nah, but I'm sure she's laying up in a hotel or something. I just hope she ain't stupid enough to pay for it herself since she had a nigga with her."

"Who did she have with her?"

"Some guy named Nate. He was Carmen's husband's best man at their wedding."

"Oh, yeah, I remember him," Rachael told me. "Oh, so she's messing with him now, huh?"

"Girl, please, that silly-ass girl doesn't know who she wants to fuck with. But I know one thing, she'd better be careful fucking all these niggas before she finds herself catching something she ain't gonna be able to get rid of."

"You ain't lying about that, because Houston has a lot of HIV cases floating around."

"Well, ain't much we can do about it. You know she's going to fuck who she wants to fuck, and do what she wants to do."

"Yeah, I know." Rachael sighed.

"Well, look, I'm going to lie back down. But call me if anything comes up, OK?"

"OK."

After Rachael and I hung up, I sat up in the bed and my head started spinning, so I lay back down. It dawned on me that I felt even more depressed now that the liquor had worn off. I still could not believe that my suspicions about Fatu were right. Fuck the shop. I wasn't planning to go anywhere that day. I had pulled my car into the garage, so nobody would know whether I was home.

I grabbed the remote and flicked on my TV. After going through every channel, I realized nothing was on, so I turned to the news channel. A newsflash came across the screen, so I turned up the volume. The young Asian reporter stood a couple feet away from a dozen police officers.

"A seventh woman was murdered last night," the reporter stated. "Police say the serial killer struck again. But this time he made his way into one of the homes on Potluck Drive of Westminster Estates."

Before the reporter could finish I sat up in my bed and turned up the volume even more.

"Police say the murder took place in the victim's home, here in the middle of this friendly neighborhood's cul-de-sac," the reporter continued. The victim, like the six others, was a young woman in her early twenties. Police say that as of right now, they have no leads, so they're asking all the women who live alone to be careful, and if anyone has any information that would link them to the killer, please call 1-800-LOCK-U-UP."

After the reporter delivered the startling news report, my stomach got weak and I felt vomit inching up my throat. I couldn't hold it in anymore. I rushed to the toilet and threw up. My head spun again and I saw black spots behind my eyes. The house they'd shown on the news was the one I had followed Fatu to. It was the same house Fatu had gone around the side of . . . and never came back out!

Oh my God! Fatu was the fucking killer!

"No . . . no . . . no!" I screamed, shaking my head in denial. It couldn't be. I threw up again, and then flopped down on my bed. It felt like someone had taken all the life out of me.

My telephone started ringing again—Fatu. My heart skipped a beat. I was so scared. I didn't know what to do. Should I let him know that I knew? Should I go to the police? So many thoughts ran through my mind. I couldn't concentrate long enough to weigh my options, so I ignored the phone and tried to think.

"Oh my God! Here I go again," I mumbled to myself because I had been through enough scandals and run-ins with crazy-ass men. It seemed like my life was destined for fucking drama, and I was sick of it. Once and for all, I knew I had to do something about it.

The first thing I did was call Nikki. It didn't matter that we were on bad terms, because right then she was the only person I had in the world. As much as I didn't want to, I knew I had to tell her what I knew about Fatu. I couldn't leave her in the dark like I did the last time. I lost my grandmother and two good friends by being selfish, and I couldn't let that happen again.

I waited patiently for Nikki to answer her cell phone, but she didn't pick up, so I left her a message. "Nikki! I know you aren't trying to talk to me right now, but I need you to call me right back as soon as you get his message. It's very important."

Turning a Deaf Ear
(Nikki Speaks)

Kira kept calling my damn phone like I wanted to talk to her ass! I just wanted her to leave me the fuck alone. I had nothing to say to her. As far as I was concerned, she no longer existed. All the shit she had taken me through, she was lucky I didn't go upside her motherfucking head. So the best thing for me to do was to stay the hell away from her. I didn't care what she had going on, because it really didn't concern me. I had my own life, and I was enjoying it without her drama.

What I should have done was tell that ho that I was sucking her fiancé's dick. I knew that would fuck up her head. She would probably want to commit suicide, which would be a good thing, but I couldn't take going to another funeral. And besides, I was truly not in the mood to buy another black dress, so I'd let her live. But what I would do was avoid her at all costs. No contact whatsoever from this day forward. As a matter-of-fact, I was going to change my number. That way I wouldn't have to worry about her at all, which would make me so happy.

After numerous calls from Kira, she finally gave up, so I got on the phone and called my girl Carmen. She and I ended up getting together for lunch. We talked about all the shit that had been going on between me and Kira. But I never once mentioned that I was fucking around with Fatu. I knew she would tell Nate in a heartbeat. Not only that, I didn't want to give her the impression that I was as sheisty as I was. Knowing her, she would probably cut me off from being her friend for fear that I would fuck her man. But I wouldn't go there. He was not my type, and plus he was too arrogant. Not only that, they had a lot of drama, so I refused to let them bring their world into mine. It just would not work.

While we were having lunch Nate called, saying he needed me, so I got the rest of my food to go and told Carmen I had to slide out of there. She understood, told me to call her later, and then we parted ways. But I never did call her. Nate had me cornered in our bedroom and I couldn't do anything else but cater to his every need. He wasn't as good as Fatu, but he would do.

Getting the Shock of My Life
(Kira Speaks)

Nikki never returned any of my phone calls. If she wanted to continue playing these stupid-ass games, I could do the same. I mean, damn, I was trying to look out for her silly ass. But if she wanted to end up one dead bitch, then I didn't care. Now that I thought about it, maybe if she did die, I would be better off. One less drama queen I'd have to worry about, and she'd be out of my hair for good. Sounded cold, but I was just now realizing that this bitch was a thorn in my side, and this town wasn't big enough for the both of us, so one of us had to go.

On the third day after my revelation about Fatu, I decided to go down to the shop because I needed to check on some things. It was a Monday evening around six PM, and the salon was closed. I drove around the block twice, just to make sure that Fatu's car wasn't parked on a side street. When I felt like the coast was clear, I parked my car and rushed inside the shop. I locked the door behind me and walked around to make sure everything was in place. I sorted through all the mail and grabbed a few things from my back office.

When I walked back to the service area I heard the doorknob

rattling as if someone was trying to get in. I was terrified. And when I saw Fatu's face through the window, my heart dropped. What was even scarier was that it had just dawned on me that I had given this nigga a key a couple of weeks after I got the locks changed, so my heart crashed into the pit of my stomach. I wanted to run out the back door, but my feet wouldn't budge. All I could do was stand there in shock and fear and watch Fatu enter the shop.

"Kira, what's the matter? Why have you been avoiding me?" he asked as he closed the door behind him.

I tried to respond, but my mouth wouldn't move.

"And what's up with that message you left me?" He continued to walk toward me.

I inched away from him, making sure I kept my eye on the baseball bat I kept beside my station.

"Fatu, a bitch called me and told me you are dealing with her," I lied, trying to throw him off. I was alone with this man, so I couldn't let on that I followed him to the house of the woman he had raped and murdered.

"Who is this woman?" Fatu growled. I could tell he was growing angrier and angrier by the minute.

"She said her name was Alana."

"Kira, you are not telling the truth. I don't know a woman with such a name." Fatu frowned. I wondered if he knew that I knew the truth. We were both trying to read each other.

"Well, that's what she told me."

"When did she call you?"

"The night I was here working on a client, and you told me you were going to be at work."

"She called here?"

"Yeah, she did. You can ask Rachael. She heard the entire

conversation." My eyes teared up. I hoped that it looked like I was getting upset at the thought that another woman who claimed to be involved with him called and harassed me. But really I was on the verge of crying because I knew my life was at stake, and I could not look that man in the eyes.

Fatu stood only about three to four inches away from me. "I don't know who that could've been, because I have never cheated on you with another woman. I would die first before I hurt you."

"Fatu, I don't have to lie." I threw out my usual attitude so he wouldn't remain suspicious. A look of ease came across his face like he was starting to feel comfortable.

"Kira, believe me, those were all lies. I wouldn't dare do such a thing. You are too precious to me. Now, if you are to be my wife, you have to trust me," Fatu said.

Hold up! Did this fucking murderer just say the word trust? "Fatu, I wanna trust you." I acted like I was torn.

"Listen, meet me at my house tonight. I have something for you," Fatu said invitingly.

I was afraid he would ask me to come over. But as scared as I was, there was one last thing I needed from his house before I could put my final plan into motion.

"OK, I'll see you tonight. But no sex, Fatu. We have to talk about this other woman," I demanded.

"That's fine, baby," Fatu relented. He kissed me on my forehead and left me standing in the middle of the salon floor. After he closed the door, I exhaled and thanked God for sparing my life once again.

When All Else Failed

(Nikki Speaks)

I'd been hanging out with Carmen, Xavier, and Nate on a regular basis since all that shit went down with me and Kira. I had to admit that I'd been really enjoying myself. The only thing that freaked me out was that every time I mentioned Neeko's name, or asked Carmen if she'd heard anything about whether he was involved in the robbery, she always found a way to avoid answering my question. All she would say was, "I told X what you said," and then she'd change the subject. She did this twice, so I vowed never to ask her about it again.

Fuck it! I didn't care what X did to Neeko. At this point in the game, I didn't even care about the jewelry I lost. To me it was just a drop in the bucket! I'd since replaced it, so I was done with that whole situation.

Aside from that, Carmen and X were cool! They weren't your typical couple. They had really competitive natures and since Xavier made a nice chunk of change out there in those streets, they walked around like they were the Russell Simmons and Kimora Lee of the hood. They both had this aura about them that made the whole world think that they were rich, and no one could fuck with them.

Carmen really made it known that she was the queen around these parts because she craved the attention. Everything she owned had to be ten times better than the next person's. I didn't pay her ass any mind, though, because she was just one of those typical chicks who ain't never had anything. You should have seen the way she rocked her Louis Vuitton bags and her iced-out bracelets. Every time I turned around, she was sporting a different style lace-front wig like she was some kind of celebrity. The jewelry her husband laced her with to replace the stones that were stolen from her at the shop was insane.

One day I met up with Carmen at her new hair salon off Ewing Drive and decided to take a ride with her out to Lincoln Park, which was a housing project located in the northeast part of Houston. X ran it like it was his very own community. Carmen told me that she had to pick up some money from him. When we pulled up outside the apartment building, X was standing by a telephone pole, talking to a couple of cats. Whatever they were talking about had all of them in an uproar. The closer we came to them, the clearer the conversation became.

"Come on, now, y'all know that nigga Kobe ain't got shit on LeBron James! Y'all know LeBron walked all over top of that nigga and made him eat dick when he made that slam dunk." Xavier demonstrated his words with hand gestures.

A couple of guys laughed while the others argued with Xavier. Carmen pulled curbside right in the middle of all the laughter and commotion. "Every time I turn around, y'all are always fussing about a game," she said.

"Ain't nobody fussing," Xavier replied. "I'm trying to school these unknowledgeable niggas about what happened in the game last night." He leaned into the car and kissed Carmen on the lips.

"Aww, ain't that cute!" I commented.

Carmen giggled and wiped saliva from the corners of her mouth.

She held out her hand to X. "You got that for me, right?"

"How much you need?"

"Give me what you think I should have." X went into his pocket and whipped out a stack of hundred-dollar bills. He divided the stack in half, gave Carmen one of the halves, and stuck the other one back into his pocket. Carmen stuck her stack inside her handbag and thanked him.

"So where y'all going?" X asked.

"To the mall."

"Weren't you just at the mall two days ago?"

Carmen sighed. "Yes, I was. But while I was there I saw a couple things that I wanted, so now I'm gonna go back and get 'em."

"I hope it ain't another damn purse. You be killing me with all those damn purses."

I chuckled. "Don't be talking about purses. Purses are like a girl's best friend."

"I thought diamonds were a girl's best friend?" Xavier asked and smiled.

"Trust me, they both go hand in hand." I looked at Carmen for a cosign.

"She ain't lying about that," Carmen agreed.

The two of them talked for a bit more and then X told Carmen to go ahead and leave. After we pulled off, Carmen told me that X didn't like it when she stayed out in the projects more than ten minutes. He said the streets weren't a place for a woman, especially his woman. I took that as a cue to tell her how my life was back in Virginia. I didn't go into lots of details about my case or the murders, but I did tell her that I was used to hanging out in that type of environment. I even told her about my two ex-boyfriends, Brian and Syncere. Carmen couldn't believe that I used to live the same exact life she was living.

"No way!"

"Whatcha mean by that?"

"I just thought that you just started fucking with hustlers when you came to H Town. Shit, I didn't know you had a track record and that you were a veteran at this shit!"

I smiled with pride. "Well, know you know. And you may not believe this either, but my last two exes had mad dough too."

"What kind of dough are you talking about?"

"I'm talking million dollar status." I lied a bit.

"Damn, your men were getting paper like that?"

"You damn right! I would not have accepted anything less."

"So, why did y'all break up?"

"Well, see, me and Brian fell apart because the feds locked his dumb ass up. And with Syncere, it was a matter of him being so damn violent. He couldn't keep his fucking hands to himself, so I had to keep it moving."

"I would've killed his ass first, and then I would've jetted on him."

"Don't worry, he got what he deserved."

"So, how was Kira living?" Carmen pried.

I could tell she would have rather talked about Kira instead of me, because Kira was a little more private and she carried herself like she had always lived a glamorous life. I was a little apprehensive about speaking on Kira at first, because I really wasn't in the mood to big up Kira's lifestyle. I mean, she wasn't all that. Then I thought, *I can say anything I want, and Carmen won't know the difference. How can she verify what I'm saying is true? I mean, it ain't like she and Kira are friends.* So I started talking my ass off.

"Did Kira ever tell you she was married?" I asked.

Surprised by my question, Carmen said, "Nah, she never mentioned it. So when was the last time you spoke to her?"

"The day she put me out."

"You haven't spoken to her since then?"

"Nope."

"You know that's not right!"

"Girl, please! Kira can kiss my ass!"

Carmen burst into laughter. "Well, whatever happened to her husband? Where is he now?"

"He got killed while he was in jail."

Even more shocked, Carmen's mouth fell wide open. "Are you kidding me?"

"No, I'm dead serious."

"What happened? Who killed him?"

"I was told that an officer on the inside did it."

"But how?"

"Well, what I was told was that Kira's husband owed some cats a lot of money, and that the only way they were gonna be able to get him was to pay somebody on the inside to clip him. And that's what they did," I exaggerated, because all in all, I didn't want her to know that Kira had his ass set up to be killed by Papi and I knew about it. That would have made me look really grimey, and I could not have that.

"Oh my God! What did Kira do? I know she must've been devastated."

"I think she knew it was going to happen," I continued to lie. "There was a lot of word on the streets before all of it went down."

"Wow! That's deep." Carmen drove with an expression of disbelief.

"Trust me, she didn't shed one tear for his ass! That nigga fucked every stylist that worked for her, and he had three kids on her with three different hood chicks from the projects. So she was glad that nigga was gone. And when she got that big-ass life insurance check in the mail, that made her life even better."

"Did they have a lot of money?"

"Yeah, he was dealing with some heavy weight."

"How much you think he was bringing in on a weekly basis?"

I thought for a moment. "Umm, probably about a couple hundred grand, if not more."

"That's it?" Carmen snorted. "The way you were talking, I thought he was making around about what X be bringing in."

"Well, see, I was just guessing because I really don't know. But I do know that they were living in a half-a-million-dollar home, and they had a lot of money stashed."

"What kind of cars were they driving?"

"Kira was driving an older model Lexus, and Ricky was driving a Benz."

"Did she have any furs or mink coats?"

"Hell yeah! She had a ton of 'em. She had all the hottest Chanel bags, Dior dresses, fur boots, diamonds necklaces, and she even slept on Versace sheets. Ricky made sure she had the flyest shit on the streets. Everybody in Virginia knew them, so they made sure they stayed on point. Bitches around our way couldn't stand her for nothing in this world. Every time I turned around different hoes would walk up in her shop and disrespect the hell out of her by airing her husband's business to everyone who was in there, saying that they slept with him and dared Kira to say or do something about it."

"What did she do?"

"Even though I can't stand the bitch right now, I will be honest and say that she didn't pay those bitches no mind. She acted like the bigger person, flaunted her big-ass diamonds, and told those hood rats that they could fuck her husband all they wanted, but they would never get his money because she held all the bank account numbers and the combination to the safe. And when she said that, those tramps were sick!"

"That was cute, but I bet she didn't have a rock like mine," Carmen commented as she admired her five-carat, princess-cut diamond ring with twenty-two side baguette-cut diamonds.

I looked at her ring and thought for a second. "Now, I ain't gonna lie, your ring is hot! But I think Kira's ring was a little bit bigger than yours. I remember her telling me her ring was a seven-carat diamond, and that Ricky paid well over fifty grand for it." The lies kept getting bigger and bigger.

"I find that hard to believe," Carmen replied with a snide look on her face.

"Well, believe it, because money was no object to Ricky, and everybody knew it." It was obvious that Carmen didn't like the idea of another woman having it going on better than her.

I looked out the window and smiled to myself. This bitch was starting to get on my fucking nerves with all this competitive bullshit. It was bad enough that I was competing with Kira, and I wasn't about to go through the same crap with this ho! Either Carmen was going to have to get a grip, or I was going to find somebody else to hang out with. Better yet, it was time to end this little party real quick and call my boo Nate. At least I didn't have to worry about him trying to outdo me. If anything, he was going to be trying to build me up. And that was exactly what I needed.

Walking Into a Death Trap

(Kira Speaks)

When I arrived at Fatu's apartment, the elevator ride that usually calmed me was making me sick. I wanted to bust the glass that surrounded me and run as fast as I could. The thing that kept me still was thoughts of the millions I could swindle from Fatu. There was no way he would deny me once I laid my cards on the table.

The elevator stopped and I exited. Fatu had the door cracked and I entered the house. Something felt eerie, like someone was watching me. Then I noticed a note on the table that sat behind the couch.

Kira, I had to run out, but I will return soon.

"Great," I whispered. Fatu wasn't home, which meant I would have enough time to find that bloody T-shirt and bounce. That was the only reason I risked coming to his house. I needed blackmail ammunition, and that shirt, which I was sure contained the DNA of one of the murdered women, was just what I needed.

I wasted no time racing upstairs. I burst into the bedroom and headed straight for Fatu's closet. Just as I suspected, his maid had not done his laundry yet. She normally washed his things once a week, on Wednesday afternoons, but every now and again she'd do them a day or so earlier if his laundry started to pile too high. The first day I saw the bloody T-shirt in the hamper was on a Thursday, and since today was Monday, there was a really good chance that the shirt would still be at the bottom of the hamper.

I scrambled through the dirty clothes like a madwoman. I ran across a couple of pairs of his dirty boxer shorts and started to sniff them, but decided against it. The smell of sex would have definitely torn my stomach all to pieces, and I couldn't afford to be in that state. After sifting through nearly every garment he had, I finally found that stained T-shirt and stuffed it into my handbag. All I had to do now was make it out of there.

"Baby, you love being in my closet," Fatu's voice boomed. I jumped so high, I could've jumped out of my skin if it were possible.

"Baby! I thought you were out. I didn't hear you come in," I gasped. Sweat beaded my hairline and my nose.

"I was."

"So what are we about to do now?"

"Make love to me," he stated in a very low tone. Fatu was acting very weird, and not only that, he could hardly look me in my eyes.

"O . . . OK. Let me just get out of these clothes," I stammered.

Fatu looked down at my purse, then turned and walked out of the closet.

Oh my God, can he see the bulge of the T-shirt through my bag? Because if he did, I know he's going to kill me for sure.

I immediately dismissed the thought when I came out of the closet and Fatu removed my clothes. He pulled me into bed with him, grabbed me in a tight embrace, and buried his face in my neck. He caressed me and kissed me gently, then forced himself inside me. I immediately threw up.

Fatu quickly scrambled off me. "Are you all right?" he asked. Concern was all over his face as he looked at the vomit splattered all over his comforter and pillowcase.

I sat up completely and wiped my mouth with the back of my hand. "It must've been something I ate earlier," I lied and moved to the other side of the bed.

"Hey, where you going?"

"I'm getting ready to get a towel or something so I can get that mess cleaned up," I explained.

"No, it's OK. Take a seat over on the chaise," he instructed me, "and I'll clean it up."

I walked over and sat down on the chaise lounge near the window and watched Fatu as he stripped the bed. I'd never seen him do any domestic duties the entire time we'd been dating, so watching him change the linens on his bed was a sight to see. Once the clean sheets and comforter were neatly in place, he escorted me back onto the bed. "Need some water?" he asked as he tucked the pillow underneath my head.

"No, I'm fine." I turned on my side.

He stuck the other sheets in the hamper and returned to the bed with me. He cuddled me in his arms, and I started to feel nauseous all over again at the mere thought of him touching me. I told him that my stomach was starting to feel upset all over again, and when he moved back from me, I turned on my stomach and looked at the wall.

We stayed this way for the entire night. I couldn't fall asleep because I kept thinking about what I had in my bag, and picturing the faces of all his victims. The very same day that I saw the news report on television, the newspaper ran a front page story with all seven women pictured on the front. I could see their faces every time I closed my eyes. I knew that the right thing to do would be to go to the police and turn in Fatu, but I also knew that I wouldn't benefit in any way from that, because even though he would be in jail, I would still be working in the shop, and his family would be after me. That settled it for me. I wouldn't go to the police at all. I would just get the money and move out of the country.

I crept out of Fatu's house before he awoke. As soon as I made it into my car, I took a minute, inhaled, exhaled, and broke down. The life I once pictured for myself was gone forever. I knew that my next communication with Fatu would be to tell him the deal.

I got home and I immediately rushed to the safe I had installed in the floor of my closet. I opened it and retrieved all of my expensive jewelry, my bonds, and some dough I had been stashing. I walked around my closet and decided which of my handbags, shoes, jeans, and coats I would take with me. I knew for damn sure I couldn't carry everything. I worked for almost an hour, loading my car with what I considered to be my essentials.

Then I drove to my Realtor Kendra Smith's office and told her to put my house up for sale, and to see what she could do with the shop. I explained to her that I would be leaving for some time, but that I would be in contact with her to collect my money once everything had been sold. She and I had grown close, so she had a lot of questions that I didn't have any answers to, especially when she asked, "Where are you going now, Kira?"

"I'm not sure, but I do know that I need to get out of here."

After I signed a contract giving her exclusive rights to orchestrate the sale of my properties, I shook her hand and left.

Putting My Plan Into Motion

(Kira Speaks)

Soon after I left Kendra's office, my Blackberry rang. It was Fatu. My heart started racing at the speed of light because I knew it was time to let the cat out of the bag, now that I had all the ammunition I needed. I took a deep breath, answered the call, and started the ball rolling.

"Hello." I answered the phone like I normally did.

"Where have you been all day? I've been trying to reach you," Fatu demanded.

"I've been running around taking care of business."

"What are you doing now?"

"Why?"

"Because I want you to meet me for dinner. Wouldn't you like to go to Benihana's tonight?"

"I'm sorry, but I am not in the mood to hang out with you tonight."

Puzzled by my response, he said, "What do you mean, you don't want to hang out with me tonight? What's the matter?"

"I'll tell you what's the matter," I snapped, just thinking about how sick he was. "I am not feeling you anymore, and the wedding is off!"

Confused by my outburst, Fatu asked, "What?"

"You heard me! I said the wedding is off."

"But I don't understand. I mean, why are you calling the wedding off?"

"Look . . ." I tried to gather my thoughts. "I know about everything. I know about the woman you raped and killed a couple nights ago."

"Kira, what are you talking about?"

"Fatu, don't play fucking games with me!" I roared. "I followed you the other night to Westminster Estates. And I saw you go inside that woman's house, so I know it was you that raped and killed her. And I got the evidence to prove it."

"You must be mistaken," he said calmly.

"Fatu, please cut the bullshit out! Now I've got that bloody T-shirt you wore on one of your other murdering sprees, and I've got two pictures of your car parked on Potluck Drive, directly in front of your last victim's house. So if you want to keep playing games like you don't know what the fuck I'm talking about, then continue to play stupid! But don't play stupid too long, because your chances of staying a free man are going to diminish by the second," I said in a stern manner.

"What do you want?" he asked.

"I want two million dollars wired to my offshore account," I said flatly.

"What!" Fatu screamed.

"You heard me! Now go in that stash you got from all that dope you sell out the back of your nightclub, and do like I just said."

"You bitch," he growled.

"No, nigga, you're the bitch!" I shot back. "Now if you disrespect me again, I'm gonna take my price up to three million!" I warned him.

Sweat dripped from my armpits. I knew that Fatu was probably wondering where I was, and that the first place he was going to look for me would be my house, but my ass was long gone from there. I was on my way to check into a hotel so that he wouldn't ever find me.

Fatu fell silent. I knew he was trying to think of the many ways he could kill me and dispose of my body. I wasn't trying to be on his time, though, so I broke into his train of thought. "So, what's it going to be?" I asked.

"How long do I have to wire this money?"

"It's one o'clock now. I'm giving you twenty-four hours to make the transaction, so make it happen."

"What am I going to get in exchange?"

"Your freedom."

"I want the shirt and the photos too."

"No problem."

"So when will I get them?"

"After I find out the money is in my account."

"OK, done." He hung up without saying another word.

When the line went dead, my nerves ricocheted all over the place. I didn't know how to take his sudden change of heart. I knew how Fatu was, and he was the type of man who did not like ultimatums. He was a very powerful and resourceful man. And with all the contacts he had around town I knew that he was going to try his best to find me no matter the cost, so I had to be on guard.

I got back on the phone and called my Realtor Kendra to ask her if she'd be able to put a hotel room for me in her name. She agreed without asking me any questions. I felt the need to give her some kind of explanation, even though it was a lie. I told her that I caught Fatu cheating on me and that I called the wedding off, which was the whole reason for me leaving, but until I actually left I didn't want him to find me. She bought the story, met me at the Marriott near the airport, and took care of everything, then we parted ways once again.

"Call me before you leave town," she said.

"I will," I assured her.

After I got inside my hotel room, I settled down and watched a few movies. Around five o'clock I ordered room service. Periodically I hopped online from my laptop to see if the transfer had been made, and when I saw that it hadn't, I wasn't a happy camper. Fatu still had some time left before I went to the police, but it wasn't as much time as he wished.

The Shit Hits the Fan

(Kira Speaks)

"Today in Houston, a beauty salon is in flames. Fire investigators say that Creative Images Salon was blown up around eleven PM tonight with an incendiary device similar to the ones used in war zones. Police and investigators are baffled by the crime, reporting that they have never seen such an explosion in a residential area, outside of war. Investigators have determined that the device was thrown through the front glass window. The salon is in ruins, and nothing could be salvaged."

My mouth fell open and I fell to my knees. My screams rang in my own ears. I felt cold all over. Fatu had blown up my fucking shop! Un-fucking-believable. This nigga wasn't playing around. I cried and cried for hours, thinking about what could possibly happen to me if my plan didn't go well. After my crying episode ended, I dried my tears and got up the nerve to call Fatu. I had to let him know that he hadn't put any fear in my heart, but he did make me very angry and I intended to get my revenge. Unfortunately for me, the bastard didn't answer, so I left him a message.

"You grimey-ass motherfucker! You think blowing up my shop was going to hurt me? You just don't know. You just bought me a nice-ass insurance check witcho stupid-ass self. And since you think you're so gangsta, your dumb ass should've waited till the daytime when my staff was in there. And since you didn't do that, now you're gonna have come harder the next time. Better yet, get my motherfucking money together or I'm gonna have somebody come after you. And instead of twenty-four hours, now you got until nine am to get me what I need, so answer your phone."

I hung up, grabbed the bottle of Grey Goose from the mini-bar, and drank it straight. The vodka burned my chest going down, but I needed it to calm my nerves. Soon I fell asleep.

A knock on the door woke me the next morning. The shit startled the hell out of me. Who in the hell could it be? No one besides Kendra knew I was there. Not even Nikki knew because I hadn't spoken to her, so my heart started beating uncontrollably. On top of that, my head was ringing like crazy from a hangover. I couldn't stand because my head would start spinning, so I lay there on the bed and prayed that whoever it was would just go away.

Five or so knocks later, a voice said, "Housekeeping,"

My heart rate slowed. "This room is still occupied," I said.

"Are you extending your stay another day?"

"I'm not sure, but I'll let you know within the next hour."

"OK, thank you." I heard her walk away. I looked at my wristwatch and noticed it was 9:52 AM. I couldn't believe that I had slept so late, but then I remembered that the Grey Goose had me comatose. I also realized that before I passed out I had left Fatu a fucked-up message on his voice mail. Since I hadn't heard my phone ring, I checked to make sure I hadn't missed his call. Just as I expected, his number was nowhere in my missed call log.

I retrieved my laptop from the foot of my bed and used my wireless broadband card to log on to the Internet again so I could check my Caribbean bank account. To my surprise, the money was there! That slummy-ass nigga must've gotten my message. He knew I was not playing with his ass, and he took heed of my advice. Thank God for that! All I had to do now was get the hell out of there.

It took me twenty minutes to get myself together. I went online and booked myself a flight to Anguilla, and then I took a quick shower and slipped into a pair of shorts and a tank top. I brushed my hair, tossed the brush inside my handbag, and stuffed my laptop back into its case. Meanwhile, my cell phone rang. I looked at the CallerID and noticed that it was Kendra, so I answered.

"Hello."

"Hey, girl, I just wanted to let you know that everything is all set. I've got a for-sale sign in front of your house as we speak, and I've been getting phone calls already. As a matter-of-fact, I'm going to have an open house tomorrow."

"Wow! So soon!" I responded with excitement.

"You're trying to get this thing sold, right?"

"Yes."

"Well then, it's not soon enough."

I chuckled. "Yeah, OK, I see what you're saying."

"Well good. I'm glad that we're on the same page. Oh, yeah, before I forget, I just got a call from your cousin Nikki asking me when you actually put your house up for sale and when was the last time I had spoken with you, which I thought was weird because you two were living together, so I assumed that she'd already know."

Shocked by Kendra's words, I said, "No, she wasn't aware. She moved out not too long ago, and we really haven't spoken since then."

"Well, that's strange, because she told me that you and her were supposed to be meeting up for lunch today, but she was having problems getting in contact with you to find out where you two would be meeting up, so I told her where you were. I hope that was fine."

My heart dropped directly to the pit of my stomach. "Did you tell her which hotel room?"

"No, but that was because I didn't remember. I did tell her that the room was in my name, though."

Oh my God! No this bitch did not just tell me that she told Nikki where the fuck I was. I can't believe this shit! I thought.

I knew Nikki wasn't inquiring about my whereabouts for herself alone. Fatu put her up to this shit, and now I had to get the hell out of there, because it would only be a matter of time before he caught me.

"How long ago was this when she called?" I asked Kendra.

"Not even fifteen minutes ago," she told me.

"OK, gotta go! I'll talk to you later," I said abruptly.

"All right, I'll call you tomorrow."

Without saying another word, I hung up. I was on the verge on panicking because I didn't know what Nikki had up her sleeve. However, I did know her well enough that I knew she had passed this information over to Fatu. I mean, why else would she call Kendra and lie about us having lunch? Shit, we weren't cool! And we would never be again, because she was a snake, and snakes couldn't be trusted.

My mind was running at one hundred miles per hour. I immediately scrambled the rest of my things together and headed out. I took the back staircase to avoid being seen on the elevator. When I got to the first floor and emerged from the side door, I headed directly to my car, which was parked next to a mini van. I hesitant at first to walk near that van, since it was parked on the driver side of my car, but then I remembered that it had been parked there last night.

I hit my car alarm button, checked my surroundings, and then I hopped inside. After I hit the automatic lock button I exhaled with relief, knowing that I was safe. But that feeling soon vanished when I saw through my rearview mirror the silhouette of someone emerge from the floor of my backseat. I gasped from fear, but before I could let out a scream, my voice died from shock.

"I see I caught you just in time," Fatu said as he sat up in the backseat.

My heart skipped a beat. Before I could unlock my driver's side door to escape, he grabbed a handful of my hair and brought my face close to his. "You thought you could blackmail me and get away with it," he whispered, his hot breath heating up my face.

"But wait," I squeaked as he squeezed my throat.

"Wait, my ass! Bitch, you're dying today," he spat in my face.

Before I could say another word, the unlock button clicked and my passenger's side door opened. It was Nikki in the flesh, standing there like she was on top of the world.

"Don't kill her here," she said. "They might have cameras around. Let's take her to the spot," she suggested.

Listening to this bitch advise Fatu about where to kill me sent chills down my spine, and my heart began to fill with pure hatred. It was apparent that this bitch had it out for me and she wanted my blood, to say the least.

"I was the last person you thought you would see, huh?" Nikki smirked as she stood there.

"Bitch, I knew you were coming! I just got off the phone with Kendra and she told me everything you said."

Nikki smiled and said, "Too bad she didn't give you a good enough head start."

"Fuck you, Nikki!"

"No, bitch! Fuck you! Because you are about to meet your maker, and after you're gone, I'm going to reverse that transfer back into Fatu's account, and then we're gonna go off and be together, and make this thing official."

I tried to break away from Fatu's grip, but the pressure he had on me wouldn't allow me to budge.

"Oh, wait a minute, bitch! Now I know you aren't trying to buck at me." Nikki was cocky. "Let her go, Fatu, so I can whip her ass for the last time."

"Shut up, Nikki!" Fatu ordered. "We don't have time for this."

"Fuck her! She needs to know that we're together. You ain't got to hide the fact that you've been fucking me real good on those nights when you weren't with her."

Nikki's words cut through me like a sharp knife and more tears spilled down my face. I was hurt, but I was angrier at the fact that I couldn't get to that whore! If I had the chance, I would've ripped off her fucking face, because, for one, she had just told me that she'd been fucking my fiancé, and two, she said that she was going to reverse the transfer and put my money back into Fatu's account. How grimey and fucked-up was that? I mean, this bitch must've really hated me or something. My own flesh and blood was down with this nigga who wanted to kill me. I knew my grandmother had to be turning in her grave.

"Didn't I just say shut up?" Fatu screamed. His focus left me for a brief second and his grip loosened around my neck, so I put a lot of force behind my body weight and tried to make my escape.

"Ugggghhhh!" I grunted with the effort as I tried to hop back out of the car, but Fatu and Nikki both grabbed me before I could get my first foot out the door. She punched me in the back of my head while he had me in a chokehold. I looked up at Nikki. "I'ma kill you, bitch!" I mumbled through my teeth.

"You can't do shit from where you are, so shut the fuck up and take this one like a woman," Nikki gloated. She sounded like a vindictive bitch. "You've escaped death twice, and now it's your time to go."

"Do you know how you sound?" I managed to say before Fatu put more pressure around my neck.

"How I sound ain't important. But the fact that Fatu knows about your past life that landed you in the Witness Protection Program is." Nikki laughed wickedly at my incredulous look. "Yeah, he knows! The secret is out. And now I'm finally going to get my life back." She reached into the car, grabbed a hold of the volume button for the radio and turned up the volume as loud as it would go. Then she went into her handbag and took out a rope, duct tape, and everything else you needed to commit a murder. All I could do was let out more tears as I pictured the breath leaving my body.

"Put that stuff away. We can't tie her up here," Fatu told Nikki.

"So what are we going to do?" she wanted to know.

"We need to knock her out so we can get out of here before someone sees us," he pointed out.

"Well, here, take the Taser gun and knock her out," she said and handed him the gun.

My mind was spinning. I didn't know what to expect from this little metal object. All I knew was that police officers used that damn thing on criminals, so it worked like magic for them. But to use it on me was a bit disturbing. Just when I was about to reason with them in hopes of finding another solution to get me from point A to point B, Fatu turned on the handheld device and stuck it right to my side.

ZZZZZZZZZZZZZZZZZZZZZZZZ! The loud, buzzing noise filled the car. It was a sound I would never forget. He moved his knee and ripped open my shirt. I kicked and wriggled my body fiercely. Fatu placed the metal tip of the machine on my chest and pressed a button that intensified the buzzing sound. *Zip! Zip! Zip!* Three hits of high-wattage electric volts hit me in the chest. My body convulsed and my eyes involuntarily rolled into the back of my head, and then everything went black.

No Way Out
(Kira Speaks)

The sound of water dripping seemed very loud as I returned to consciousness. I opened my battered eyelids and squinted to see where I was. It was dark and the smell of mold hung in the air, so I knew I was no longer inside my car. I fell in and out of consciousness for what seemed like eternity. After a while, I heard Nikki's voice. She was trying to whisper.

"I went through her whole house and I couldn't find it," she said.

"Why the fuck not? Her house isn't but so big!" Fatu screamed.

"What else do you want me to do?" Nikki asked, her voice wavering.

"Just know that if I go down, so do you. Remember, you were the one who got Crissy and those women to trust me. You were the reason I got inside their houses. You were there when I murdered them. And you held the video camera," he said through clenched teeth.

I almost threw up when I heard his words. Nikki was an accessory to all those murders. Not only that, but it became clear to me that Nikki would do anything for a man, or for what she perceived to be a man.

"We can't kill her until we know that we have the information we need," Fatu said, pacing.

"Why can't we just leave town?" Nikki proposed. "You got more than enough money, and I have access to Kira's accounts. So after we get rid of her, we're gonna have everything we need."

"No! You don't understand. I can't leave my family, so this whole thing has to go away. If we find the evidence, we can kill her and move on like nothing ever happened."

As I listened to him, I understood he was making it clear to Nikki that he was not going to be with her either. I doubted that Nikki understood that Fatu had just used the both of us, and she fell for his charm and his money. She had betrayed the only best friend she had left in the world—me!

I knew they would never find the evidence. On my way to the hotel I had stopped by my bank and locked the T-shirt—stuffed into a manila envelope—in my safe deposit box that, thankfully, Nikki knew nothing about. In fact, I got the deposit box right after I put her ass out of my house, so I had no worries about her finding it. If anything, the police would probably find it first. Since I had a note attached to it, it wouldn't be hard for them to link Fatu to the murder. The only thing I didn't include in the note was that Nikki was an accessory to those women's murders, because I didn't know that then.

What in the hell was she thinking? How could she have befriended those women and then let Fatu rape and kill them while she videotaped it? That shit was insane. I couldn't fathom the thought of any woman doing that for a man. Fatu's dick wasn't that good, and I knew he wasn't selling her the dream that he'd marry her instead of me, so what was her problem? Whatever it was, it was serious and she needed to see a psychiatrist quickly. I suddenly heard footsteps coming in my direction.

"Kira, get up!" Fatu lifted my chin and shined a bright light into my eyes. The methods he used led me to believe that he had performed acts of torture before. Maybe he was a guerilla rebel in Africa, and that was why he had so much money. Fatu had some skills that only those types of people would have.

I moaned. Fatu took my hand, forcefully placed it on the table, and used a pair of pliers to snatch off one of my fingernails.

"Where is the T-shirt?" Fatu asked while Nikki dug her nails into my wrists. "Where is it, Kira?" Fatu screamed. I still did not answer.

Nikki was beginning to grow angrier by the moment. "Kira, just tell him. You're gonna die anyway," she urged.

I rolled my eyes. Nikki had betrayed me in the worst way. She knew that I had her as the beneficiary on all of my bank accounts, my house, and the shop. Not only did she stand to get the two million that Fatu had put in my account to make me think the deal had gone through, but she also stood to receive the insurance money from the shop explosion. Nikki was going to make a good three to four million if I died today. And with that alone, I vowed not to utter a word.

Continuously they tortured me. I shrieked in horrible pain. Tears rolled down my face and the only thing that kept me alive was the fact that they didn't know what I had done with that evidence.

Nikki smiled like she was enjoying seeing me in pain. "Don't cry now, Ms. Bad Ass! You supposed to be hard, remember?"

All I could think about through the pain was that Nikki was in over her head, and sadly, she didn't even realize it. Just as Fatu prepared to pull out another fingernail, I heard a *BANG!* I couldn't tell where they sound had come from, because the light was still shining in my eyes.

"What was that?" Nikki asked nervously. My heart jumped in my chest. *That has to been the police!* I grew excited. For the moment I felt like my life would be spared.

"Turn off the light," Fatu instructed frantically. We must have been in an abandoned building of some sort because of the acoustics. Every word echoed very loudly.

BANG! I grew more and more excited, waiting to hear the words, "FREEZE! POLICE!" I never thought I'd be happy to see any police. I could hear Fatu and Nikki scrambling in the dark like the rats that they were. I was in too much pain to care what they did anymore. I tried to focus on the thought of some cop tossing me over his shoulder and running out the door, saving me.

Suddenly I heard footsteps. Fatu heard them too because he pulled a gun from his waistband, but then the footsteps stopped. There was dead silence. I could hear Nikki breathing hard. I remained still. Fatu decided to turn on the light to see what was going on. *Click.* A snub-nosed Berretta was right in his face.

"Drop the gun," a man instructed. Fatu complied. His gun and his last hope hit the floor with a thud while Nikki immediately began to sob. Apparently she knew it was all over for her. I, on the other hand, became ecstatic because I knew that I was about to regain my freedom. God definitely had other plans for my life.

Throughout all this, I kept my eyes closed tightly because I didn't want to witness shit. I wanted to wait until everything was over so I wouldn't carry the bad memories of this event with me for the rest of my life. My legs felt numb where they were duct-taped to the chair, and I could not have moved them even if I wanted to. All of the electricity that had been surging through my body made me weak. I felt like I was one-hundred-years-old.

"I've been waiting for this moment for a very long time," the man said. Fatu remained silent. I frowned. The voice I'd just heard was the voice of an African. Whoever that man was hadn't asked Fatu and Nikki to freeze or get down on the floor, so he wasn't a cop. *What the hell is really going on?* I wondered.

"You know it ends here now, right?"

I finally recognized the voice. It was Bintu! Why was he there? What in the hell was about to end?

"You don't have the heart to kill me. You were weak then, and you are weak now," Fatu said, his voice laced with pride.

"Cousin, don't let him speak to you like that! Kill them now!" another voice commanded. Bintu had one of his soldiers with him and they were all related to each other. Whatever was going on had to do with some disloyalty in the family.

"Are you kidding me?" Fatu chuckled as he addressed the second man. "Kofi, he's weak. He's a fucking coward!"

Bintu laughed. "Yes, I am a coward, but you are sick. We found the blackmail letter Kira sent you. And the part that disgusted me the most was how she laid out all the evidence she had on you to link you to that last murder. She really had you by the balls, and she could have taken you down with no problem. But if we would have allowed that to happen, it would have jeopardized our entire family and all our export businesses. Remember, the only reason you were sent to America was because you were doing the same thing to the women in our nearby villages. If Father hadn't paid off the Nigerian authorities to keep them from throwing you into prison for the rest of your life, you would be living as a peasant right now."

"You don't know shit about me!" Fatu roared.

"I know enough to know that you repulse me. You were not even smart enough to change your pattern from the one you used back home. That is the sickest thing ever." Bintu cocked his gun and prepared to fire.

Fatu hocked spit onto the floor. "Father is going to have your head for this!"

"Who do you think ordered this?" Bintu asked.

Fatu fell silent. My heart dropped when I heard a third voice—Mr.

Oduka. "Pray for your soul, son," he said and pulled the trigger. *Boom!*

It took everything within me not to scream. I wanted to run my ass out of there because these people were serious.

"What do you want to do about her?" Bintu asked.

"Now you know we can't have any witnesses," Mr. Oduka replied. His footsteps echoed in the distance as he walked away.

"Please don't kill me!" Nikki sobbed even louder as she pleaded for her life, but it was too late. Bintu fired, and I heard her hit the ground, screaming. Although she had watched me get tortured and was going to have me killed over jealousy and greed, I had a hard time dealing with her execution. I was literally hurting inside and wanted to scream, but I knew I couldn't. If Bintu knew that I was still alive, I was going to be his next victim.

I continued to play the part of a corpse. *BOOM!* I heard Nikki's body jerk on the floor and then the screaming stopped. I knew she was dead.

"Kofi, go get Matthew and Thomas so you guys can clean this up," Bintu instructed.

"All right." Kofi left.

I heard Bintu walk toward me and I was about to freak out. I had no idea what he was about to do, and since I wanted to stay alive, I continued to pretend like I was dead.

He stopped and stood still. I figured he was trying to see if I was still breathing, so I held my breath and prayed to God that he'd give me the strength to last as long as I could. A few seconds passed before Bintu turned and walked away. I exhaled slowly, but I never opened my eyes until I heard a door close.

Finally I let out a huge sigh of relief. I couldn't believe that I'd survived another bloody massacre. I waited a few minutes more before I opened my eyes, but I was not prepared for what I saw. Fatu and Nikki lay in their own pools of blood with gunshot wounds to their heads.

I leaned over and vomited right on the spot before I realized that wasn't a very smart thing to do. But how in the hell could I have prevented it? I couldn't dwell on it because I had to get the hell out of there before Kofi and those other two niggas came back and saw that I was alive.

I managed to wiggle and squirm my way out of the rope and the duct tape. When I finally was able to stand up, my legs felt like achy logs. My insides hurt, plus my fingers were bleeding profusely where the nails had been ripped out. I felt like I was dying slowly, but I wasn't about to let that slow me down.

I almost shat on myself when a hand grabbed me around my ankle. I screamed and saw that Fatu was clinging to my ankle for dear life. I nearly lost it.

"Please help me," he gasped. Blood bubbled through his lips.

I couldn't respond to his plea. I was completely at a loss for words and all I wanted to do was get out of there. I shook him off frantically and sprinted away as quickly as I could. When I got to the door, I snatched it open and froze when I saw Bintu blocking the entrance. My first instinct was to turn around and run in the opposite direction, but that would have been a dummy move because there was nowhere for me to escape. I stood and awaited my fate.

"Going somewhere?" Bintu asked. His face showed no sign that he was about to let me go. I couldn't speak to save my life. Literally. "Where is the evidence you have?" he asked.

"I put it away in a safe place," I croaked.

"Where is this safe place?"

"Are you going to kill me if I take you to it?" My voice trembled.

"Are you going to give me the evidence?" he asked.

"I will, if you let me live."

"What guarantees will I have that you aren't going to go to the police?"

"The only thing you have is my word," I said in a low, weak whisper.

"I will accept that, but you're going to also have to give me your word that you're going to get out of town as well."

"I was already prepared to do that," I assured him. "I have a two o'clock flight leaving from Houston tomorrow afternoon."

Bintu nodded. "Where is this safe place?" he asked again.

"OK. I need to go to the Bank of Commerce." What did I have to lose at this point? I was going to give them what they wanted in exchange for my freedom. I had had enough.

Bintu frowned. "Well, it's too late to do anything tonight. The bank is closed, so we will get up early in the morning to take care of that."

"What's gonna happen to me until then?" I asked nervously.

"You will come with me."

That gave me an uneasy feeling. What I really wanted to do was go my own way and meet up the next day, but I knew that wasn't an option. Bintu wasn't going to give me an opportunity not to show. A bleak expression crossed my face. The only thing I could say was, "Where are you taking me?"

"To a safe place. You will be fine. No one is going to hurt you. You have my word on that." Even though Bintu seemed like he could be trusted, I still wasn't comfortable going with him. But what other choice did I have? He'd already made up his mind, and I couldn't muster up any strength to fight him and try to escape, so I just gave in and allowed him to escort me to his vehicle.

During the drive I asked, "What made you stick around? Did you know that I was still alive?"

Bintu nodded. "Yes, I knew."

"Well, why did you leave me sitting there?"

"I had my reasons." He continued to look straight ahead.

"Can I ask you another question?"

Bintu sighed. "Sure."

"What are you going to do with Fatu's and my cousin's bodies?"

"I can't discuss what we're going to do with Fatu's body, but as far Nikki's body, I can say that we're going to put it somewhere visible for the police to find her. I'm sure your family would want to have a proper burial for her."

I nodded and began to think about how my aunt and uncle were going to take Nikki's death. There was no question in my mind that they were going to blame it on me, so there was absolutely no need for me to call them with the news, or for that matter, attend her funeral. If all went well tomorrow, I was going to give Bintu the package from my safe deposit box and then I was going to leave this country, never to return again.

When we arrived at Bintu's new place, I was given some food and then he arranged for me to get some medical attention. The family's doctor stitched up my cuts and wrapped my ribs before two women dressed in African garb bathed me and gently brushed my hair. I almost forgot where I was until they showed me where I was going to sleep. The room was warm and inviting, but I had let my guard down enough, so I knew I could not fall asleep. The hours passed like days. I had been captured and tortured for twenty-six hours, and I had not slept a wink. Although I was weak and dead tired, now wasn't the time to lose focus.

When the morning came, I quickly got dressed. Before I could leave the bedroom, there were two knocks on the door, then Bintu walked in. "Good morning." He smiled as he walked toward me. I never realized how attractive Bintu was until that moment. When Nikki and

I met him and Fatu, I had focused solely on Fatu. Fatu seemed to have the most money, he was the flashier of the two, and he was the one who aggressively pursued me. Bintu was always so low-key, but apparently he was the better of the two men in the end.

I thought about Nikki and the deterioration of our relationship. It had been coming for a long time, and when she found out that Bintu actually worked for Fatu, that sent shock waves through whatever ties we had left. That was when the tension between us started increasing, and our relationship became too frayed to be repaired. Too bad things ended the way they did, but I had absolutely no control whatsoever over her destiny. Nikki chose her path, and all I could do was move on and pray that today went as smoothly as I hoped it would.

"How are you feeling, Kira?"

"Better," I said apprehensively.

"Are you ready?"

"Yes, I'm ready." I suddenly remembered that I needed identification. "Hey, I'm gonna need my laptop and handbag with all my important documents in it, like my driver's license, credit cards, and my passport."

"I retrieved all of your belongings from Fatu's car last night, and they will be waiting for you when you get into my car."

"OK." I followed him outside.

Kofi and Matthew both sat in the back seat of Bintu's BMW. My heart nearly jumped out of my chest when I saw them. I wanted so badly to ask why they were accompanying us on this trip, but then I figured I'd probably be wasting my breath. I got in on the passenger side. The ride to the bank was silent. I looked out the window at the city of Houston. I knew in my heart that this would be my last ride through here. Whether Bintu would betray me and kill me, I didn't know, but either way, I was leaving here.

A Sticky Situation
(Kira Speaks)

While Bintu stood watch over me, I slowly pulled up the metal lever and opened the box. It seemed like he and I both had stopped breathing because it was so quiet in the room. I exhaled and my shoulders slumped as I stared down at the manila envelope. Tears ran down my face at the knowledge that my life had come down to this—a plain white T-shirt smeared with a helpless woman's blood. I looked up at Bintu as he smiled. I pushed the box in his direction and he snatched the envelope from the box.

"Thank you, Kira. You have done an honorable thing." His accent was thicker and more pronounced, like he had just arrived from Africa.

"You're welcome," I said. I didn't know what else to say.

"Here. This is yours." He handed me an envelope. I looked at him, and looked back at the envelope. "Take it and get out of here," he ordered.

I opened the envelope and found a cashier's check in the amount of five million dollars. I was stunned. I'd never seen so many zeros in my entire life!

"Oh my God, Bintu! What is this for?"

"Because you kept your word, and in this life, whether you are here in the US or anywhere else in the world, your word and your loyalty are all you have," Bintu explained.

Before I responded to his financial gesture, my mind immediately reflected back on the day I stood in front of Papi inside of his store front business and accepted that money from him after I had informed him that my late husband was trying to set him up with the FEDS in exchange for his freedom. I didn't know it then, but I had signed my death certificate once the hit was put out of Ricky and his partner and my secret lover Russ. And if the game was still played the same way, I would be doing the exact same thing all over again by accepting this money, and I couldn't do that. So without further delay, I shoved the check back into the envelope and handed it back to Bintu.

"I can't accept this," I told him.

"Why not?" he asked.

"Because I cannot be bought. What I did for you was merely an even exchange for my life, and you cannot put a price tag on that. So once I walk out these doors, I will be a free woman."

Bintu smiled and stuck the envelope back in the inside of his jacket pocket. "Very well," he said and then he gave me a head nod of respect.

As I began to close the safety deposit box and lock it, Bintu proceeded to the door of the confined room.

"If you like I can have a car take you wherever you want to go," he offered.

"No, that's OK. I'd rather take a cab."

"As you wish," he replied and then he walked out.

I held my hand up to my heart and exhaled. I was finally free! Well, at least for that very moment, and I intended to keep it that way.

After I lifted the safety deposit box in my hand, I slid it back into the slot and walked toward the front entrance of the bank. I took a deep breath and prayed a very small prayer that God would allow me to get me out of this country alive. I promised him that if he gave me one more chance to get my life right, I would, and that I would pick up my Bible every day and read it. I ended with the words, "In Jesus's name," and then walked outside.

I flagged the first taxi I saw and instructed the driver to take me to the airport. I sat quietly in the backseat during the entire drive because I was leery of everything around me, especially the driver. I figured since Bintu knew I was going to take a taxi to the airport, then he could have had this guy posted up somewhere, waiting for me to come out of the bank. I moved closer to the door in case I needed to jump out at any given moment.

Periodically I looked out of the back window to see if anyone was following me. Although it didn't seem like there was someone on my tail, I told myself that I still needed to keep my guard up.

Finally we pulled up to the curb outside Southwest Airlines. I paid the driver and quickly got out of the car.

"Need some help with your bags?" the driver asked.

"No, I got it," I assured him. I didn't want him touching my bags. He could stick any kind of small tracking device on them. Besides, I only had a small carry-on and a duffel bag. I didn't have time to go back home and pick up the rest of my shit I had packed, so what I had was the bare minimum.

The driver stepped back and allowed me to go on my merry way, and I was off to my new life.

A Whole New World

(Kira Speaks)

When I arrived in Anguilla, the sound of a steel drum danced in my ears. All of the brightly colored buildings lightened my mood. I received many hellos and smiles from the natives. As I left the airport, I smiled to myself and headed straight to the bank. Inside I looked around at all of the bright, pastel colors, and at all of the happy islanders. I withdrew enough money to stay in a hotel until I could find a place to live.

Anguilla was a much-needed change of scenery. I loved the smell of the ocean and the sound of the waves. I thought about Nikki and everything that had transpired between us. It saddened me that we could've shared all of this together, but she let greed and jealously blind her. At times I even found myself missing her. It didn't matter that things got really ugly in the end, because when I thought about the good times we had, they truly outweighed the bad ones. I shook my head, willing myself to stop thinking about the past. It wasn't doing me any good. Besides, I was trying to move forward, and I couldn't do that if I continued to hang on to the past.

Up in my hotel room, I jumped onto the soft, plush bed which was dressed in all white linen with what seemed like about fifty pillows. I took a strawberry from the fruit basket on the nightstand and bit into it.

"Ahhhh, the taste of serenity," I said. I rushed around the suite like a kid in a candy store. There were huge mirrors everywhere, a soaker bathtub, a glass-encased shower, and a large balcony overlooking the ocean. I bet the sunrises and sunsets were better than the ones I'd loved watching so much from the balcony in Fatu's apartment.

The next few weeks on Anguilla were amazing. I never knew all of the things you could do alone when you loved yourself. I just took the time to get to know Kira. After a month of house shopping, I decided to make a purchase. As I was hustling out of the hotel to sign the final paperwork on the house, I bumped into a chick.

"Excuse me," I apologized. When the woman turned around, I nearly fainted. It was Frances, Ricky's baby's mama, the very bitch I had it out with at the Taco Bell restaurant and couldn't stand to be around.

My mind started racing like crazy and my heart started beating rapidly because she and I had not seen each other since my disappearance. And now here I was in another country like everything was all well and good. Really and truly, I didn't want to come off as the bitch I could be, so I stood there and waited for her to respond. She grabbed her handbag and pulled it up on her shoulder.

"Well, well, well, if it ain't Ms. Kira, VA's biggest snitch!" she said. "Word was on the streets that you came back from the dead, but I didn't believe 'em. But I guess they were right."

I smiled, trying to play if off. "Nice to see you finally got with a nigga that would take you to a hotel outside the state of Virginia. I mean, you know this is unusual for you, coming from the projects and all. I'm so used to seeing you fuck with those block hustlers, so it's really weird seeing you out here!"

"I fucked your husband, didn't I?"

"Yes, you did, but what did you get out of it other than a bastard child?"

Frances blew her top. "Bitch, don't worry about my daughter! She's not a bastard! But what you need to worry about is Ricky's peoples, because they are looking for your grimey ass! And I can't wait to let them know I saw you."

I smiled and said, "Well, while you at it, tell 'em I said hi too."

"You think you're being smart, huh?"

I ignored her question and continued to smile at her. I knew this would piss her off.

"Bitch, don't keep smiling at me! We ain't cool! You had my fucking baby daddy killed! And now you're walking 'round here like your shit don't stink."

I plastered another fake smile on my face. "Last time I checked, my shit didn't stink! But as far as me having my husband killed, that's a damn lie! So whoever told you that bullshit is a liar! And tell 'em I said so too."

"I'ma do more than that, ho!" she said and took a couple of steps toward me.

I took a couple of steps away from her. "Frances, you better think real hard before you run up on me this time. I've been through a lot of bullshit these last couple of months, so I have a lot of aggression built up inside me. And when I finally release some of it, I'm gonna come hard," I warned her.

"Bitch, do you think I care about your aggression? I will stomp your ass right here and now!" she roared back and took a couple more steps toward me.

Everybody and their mama stood around and watched to see what was going to happen next. But I guess the cat she was with refused to see our little gripping session escalate to higher heights because he dropped everything he had in his hands and grabbed her by her arm. "Come on, Fran, it ain't worth it. We came here to have a nice time, so let's go."

"Fuck that! This bitch needs to get what she deserves."

"And she will. But now ain't the time," he replied.

Frances looked at me with vengeance and I gave her that same look right back. Shit, who the fuck did she think she was? I didn't ask for none of that drama I went through with Ricky and Fatu. I'd always been the quiet, laid back chick. But those characteristics of mine never seemed to work in my favor. For some reason I always seemed to attract assholes for niggas. So why did she feel like I got what I deserved, like I was some snake-ass bitch? I was a good girl. Fuck them! I didn't have time to keep listening to this shit!

"Listen to your man! He's got more sense than you'll ever have!" I finally told her and then I walked off.

I immediately grabbed a taxi. "Take me to the Orchard Villas, please," I instructed the driver. I turned around to look out of the back window and noticed that Frances had pulled out her cellular phone and dialed someone's number as she watched the taxi take me away. That shit really scared the hell out of me. I didn't know who the hell she was calling, but I did know that it was somebody from Ricky's family, and I wasn't about to stick around to find out what was being said. I also decided that I wasn't going to let this guy take me straight to my destination. "You know what, sir? I changed my mind. I'm not going to the Orchard Villas, so could you take me to another hotel?" I asked.

"Which one? You know that there are dozens on this island," he replied in a thick Anguillan accent.

"Sir, it really doesn't matter. Just take me to the nicest one."

"You got it." He pressed down on his accelerator.

It took the taxi driver less than ten minutes to get me to another hotel. I paid him, got out of the car, waited for him to pull off, and then got right back into another taxi, which took me home to Orchard Villas. I could not take any chances.

I couldn't say how long Frances and her new hustler boyfriend were going to be in this country, but I knew that it would be wise for me to stay out of sight. And that's exactly what I did. God knows that it would be one sad day if I were walking down the beach and one of Ricky's people ran up on me and tried to lay my ass out with a bullet straight to the head. But what would really be fucked up was that no one out here would help me, and my life would be over just like Nikki's.

Since I couldn't fathom that ever coming into play, I was just gonna have to live the rest of my life looking over my shoulders. Truth be told, it won't be hard to do. It seemed like I'd been running for my life forever and a day. I had enough practice hiding out from those Russian cats thinking they were the feds, so this time would be a slam dunk. Well . . . hopefully!

MELODRAMA PUBLISHING ORDER FORM
WWW.MELODRAMAPUBLISHING.COM

Title	ISBN	QTY	PRICE	TOTAL
Wifey	0-971702-18-7		$15.00	$
I'm Still Wifey	0-971702-15-2		$15.00	$
Life After Wifey	1-934157-04-X		$15.00	$
Still Wifey Material	1-934157-10-4		$15.00	$
Sex, Sin & Brooklyn	0-971702-16-0		$15.00	$
Histress	1-934157-03-1		$15.00	$
Den of Sin	1-934157-08-2		$15.00	$
Eva: First Lady of Sin	1-934157-01-5		$15.00	$
Eva 2: First Lady of Sin	1-934157-11-2		$15.00	$
The Madam	1-934157-05-8		$15.00	$
Shot Glass Diva	1-934157-14-7		$15.00	$
Dirty Little Angel	1-934157-19-8		$15.00	$
Cartier Cartel	1-934157-18-X		$15.00	$
In My Hood	0-971702-19-5		$15.00	$
In My Hood 2	1-934157-06-6		$15.00	$
A Deal With Death	1-934157-12-0		$15.00	$
Tale of a Train Wreck Lifestyle	1-934157-15-5		$15.00	$
A Sticky Situation	1-934157-09-0		$15.00	$
Jealousy	1-934157-07-4		$15.00	$
Life, Love & Lonliness	0-971702-10-1		$15.00	$
The Criss Cross	0-971702-12-8		$15.00	$
Stripped	1-934157-00-7		$15.00	$
The Candy Shop	1-934157-02-3		$15.00	$
Cross Roads	0-971702-18-7		$15.00	$
A Twisted Tale of Karma	0-971702-14-4		$15.00	$

(GO TO THE NEXT PAGE)

MELODRAMA PUBLISHING ORDER FORM
(CONTINUED)

Title/Author	ISBN	QTY	PRICE	TOTAL
Up, Close & Personal	0-971702-11-X		$9.95	$
Menace II Society	0-971702-17-9		$15.00	$
			Subtotal	
			Shipping**	
			Tax*	
	Total			

Instructions:

*NY residents please add $1.79 Tax per book.

**Shipping costs: $3.00 first book, any additional books please add $1.00 per book.

Incarcerated readers receive a 25% discount. Please pay $11.25 per book and apply the same shipping terms as stated above.

Mail to:

MELODRAMA PUBLISHING

P.O. BOX 522

BELLPORT, NY 11713